"I do apologize. I wasn't very professional last night."

"No, you weren't," Hunt told her, his tone measured and calm. "You weren't wearing any shoes—and you have pretty toes by the way. You tossed back superb whiskey like it was Kool-Aid, fed me chocolate and invited me into your bed."

Yeah, she remembered. She'd been there.

"I'll completely understand if you don't want to proceed with this meeting," Adie said, her words stiff.

Hunt had the temerity to flash a megawatt grin. "No, you're here and I'll listen to your pitch. But..."

Adie held her breath as he walked across the room to stand in front of her, hands in his pockets, completely at ease. He stared down at her. "But, at some time in the future, rain or shine, hail or hellfire, we will pick up where we left off last night."

Dear Reader,

Merry Christmas from my family to yours.

This story takes its inspiration from a documentary I recently watched about the lives of the superrich and the people who supply them with the best of the best, be it food or clothes or Christmas ornaments!

Adie Ashby-Tate has left London to spend the weeks preceding Christmas in New York City to see if it is feasible to establish a Manhattan branch of her private concierge company. She sets up an indoor market to display her one-of-a-kind gifts and meets a mystery man whom she very uncharacteristically propositions. Fate intervenes before they share more than a kiss, and Adie is relieved. She no longer uses men as a distraction to get her through the Christmas season. She is in Manhattan to acquire clients, including, hopefully, Hunter Sheridan, owner of a chain of sports stores.

Except that Hunter is the guy she kissed at her indoor market...

A fling is all they can have, right?

Happy reading!

Joss

Xxx

Connect with me on Facebook (josswoodauthor), Twitter (@josswoodbooks), BookBub (joss-wood) or my website (josswoodbooks.com).

JOSS WOOD

—

HOT HOLIDAY FLING

HARLEQUIN®
DESIRE™

Recycling programs
for this product may
not exist in your area.

ISBN-13: 978-1-335-20952-8

Hot Holiday Fling

Copyright © 2020 by Joss Wood

This edition published by arrangement with Harlequin Books S.A.

For questions and comments about the quality of this book, please contact us at CustomerService@Harlequin.com.

Harlequin Enterprises ULC
22 Adelaide St. West, 40th Floor
Toronto, Ontario M5H 4E3, Canada
www.Harlequin.com

Printed in U.S.A.

Joss Wood loves books and traveling—especially to the wild places of southern Africa and, well, anywhere. She's a wife, a mom to two teenagers and slave to two cats. After a career in local economic development, she now writes full-time. Joss is a member of Romance Writers of America and Romance Writers of South Africa.

Books by Joss Wood

Harlequin Desire

Hot Holiday Fling

Murphy International

One Little Indiscretion
Temptation at His Door
Back in His Ex's Bed

Love in Boston

Friendship on Fire
Hot Christmas Kisses
The Rival's Heir
Second Chance Temptation

Visit her Author Profile page at Harlequin.com, or josswoodbooks.com, for more titles.

You can also find Joss Wood on Facebook, along with other Harlequin Desire authors, at Facebook.com/harlequindesireauthors!

One

Adie Ashby-Tate was done—for this evening at least.

In a small but exquisitely decorated conference room in the iconic Grantham-Forrester hotel on 5th Avenue in the heart of Manhattan, Adie waved goodbye to her last guest and allowed her smile to fade.

She gripped the edge of her main display table, thankful for the empty room now that all the millionaires and billionaires who'd attended her "Christmas Indoor Market" had left. She loved interacting with clients and showing them her carefully chosen wares, but keeping the charm flowing for four or more hours was exhausting.

Because her feet were aching, Adie kicked off her heels and sank her feet into the expensive carpet. She looked around, pleased she'd managed to capture the essence of a snowy European Christmas market in the small ballroom. She'd strung fairy lights, the ten-foot Christmas tree in the corner was draped with fake snow and a diffuser released hints of hot choco-late, pinecones and cider. She'd dropped the temper-ature to just this side of chilly to echo the sharp bite of a snow-tinged winter's night and she'd propped a snowboard and skis against a papier-mâché replica of a horse-drawn buggy.

The room suggested wealth, but more importantly, romance and the spirit of Christmas. The costs in-volved made her eyes water, but setting the scene, drawing in her clients and then transporting them to a simpler time was worth every penny and the hours of backbreaking work.

Still holding onto one of her display tables—covered in an expensive rich red velvet—Adie stared down at her burgundy-tipped toes and rotated her head from side to side. In a moment she'd move to the bar and pour herself a much-deserved drink, a reward for a job exceptionally well done.

An evening that ended with a book full of or-ders could be termed only successful, and her arti-sanal, superbly talented suppliers were going to be very, very pleased with her work tonight. More or-ders would come. Her gifts were one of a kind and the very rich liked nothing more than rarity and ex-clusivity.

After this event, Adie was spending the run-up

to Christmas in New York City to see whether there was scope for her to open a branch of Treasures and Tasks in Manhattan and to ascertain whether she and Kate—a new friend she'd met through one of her clients—could work together. She needed more than a few orders before she decided to sink a lot of cash into expanding into one of the most expensive cities in the world. So she'd spend the next three weeks working out of New York, testing the market while juggling requests from her existing clients in London and all over the world.

As an exclusive, private concierge who dealt only with very high net worth individuals, Christmas was Adie's busiest season. But she wanted, and needed, every moment of her days filled, especially at this time of year. This was the time of the year when the ghosts of the past—Christmas and his friends—decided to drop by and harangue her and she'd prefer to be too busy to pay them any attention.

She'd be exhausted in January, but being distracted was worth the price.

Adie looked at her tables. More than half a million pounds worth of inventory sat on the exquisitely decorated tables—from jewel-encrusted bottle stoppers to gold plated memory sticks—but because some of the richest people had the stickiest fingers, she needed to count the inventory and then pack everything away. It would take a few hours.

Tomorrow she had a series of meetings with potential clients, but the one guy Kate never stopped talking about—an old friend of Kate's whom she called "the most reluctant influencer" on Earth—hadn't pitched. Turned out, Adie hadn't needed his support. Tonight had been a raging success.

Adie heard the rap of knuckles on the partially open ballroom door and swiftly turned. This was an upmarket hotel with good security, but being burgled was always a possibility.

The man in the doorway was doing a damn fine job of stealing her breath.

Adie placed her hand on her sternum and told herself she was an idiot for feeling lightheaded. He was just a man, flesh and blood…

But…*what* a man!

He was so tall he had to duck his head to walk through the door. Wide shoulders, long muscular legs and what had to be a washboard stomach under the mint green button-down shirt tucked into a pair of plain black pants. He held a battered leather jacket in his clutched fist. His body was off the charts hot, but it was his face that held Adie's attention.

A young Cary Grant, maybe… But then she quickly decided he wasn't classically handsome enough for the comparison to work. He had the broad forehead and the strong chin, but his nose was a little too hooked, his stubble too thick to carry off Grant's urbane, man-about-town look. No, this man belonged in action, like her all-time favorite Hollywood hotties, Gerard Butler and Tom Hardy.

"Ma'am, he was on the guest list so I let him up. I hope that's okay?"

Adie pulled her eyes off Mr. Delicious to look at the security guard. When she processed the amusement in Dan's eyes at her slack-jawed reaction to her guest, she straightened her spine and told herself to act her age. Many billionaire princes and A-list movie stars were her clients. She was not normally this easily impressed.

Meeting those light eyes—fog blue or silver?—under those straight thick brows, a shade lighter than the burnt sugar color of his hair, she felt pinned to the floor, but finally managed to pull a polite smile onto her face. "Good evening. You're a couple of hours late, but you're welcome to take a quick look if you don't mind me packing away behind you."

"I should've been here earlier, but I was unavoidably detained."

His voice was as rich as the dark chocolate tart she'd consumed in a tiny restaurant in the French Quarter of New Orleans last year. But within the richness, Adie heard exhaustion. Frankly, the man looked like he needed a drink. She gestured to the small bar tucked into the corner. "Can I offer you a drink?"

"God, yes. Please. Whiskey if it is available."

Adie smiled at his enthusiasm and walked, still barefoot, to the bar. She glanced down at her feet and shrugged. He was four hours late, she was packing up and her three-inch slingbacks were beautiful but torturous so he'd have to live with her bare feet.

And judging by the glance he'd directed at her legs, bare under the edges of a red cocktail dress hitting her legs midthigh, he rather liked what he saw.

It had been a while since she'd come across a man who made her feel both hot and shivery. It was a delightful feeling but, she cautioned herself, also a dangerous one.

Be careful, Adie.

Adie held two bottles in the air. "Bourbon or Scotch?"

"Scotch, please. On the rocks, if there is ice."

Appreciating his choice of a twelve-year-old whiskey, Adie poured a healthy amount into two glasses and lifted the lid on an ice bucket. Using silver tongs, she picked up ice cubes and dumped a couple each in the crystal tumblers before walking back over to him. Without her heels, the top of her head reached only his collarbone and next to him she felt dainty and deliciously feminine.

Adie handed him the glass and his fingers slid over hers, sending a delicious stream of "oh, yeah" up her arm and causing her nipples to contract. Heat pooled between her legs and she felt both languorous and hyped. Adie stared down at her fingers, still wrapped around the glass, bracketed by his darker ones. She wanted to see, and feel, his fingers cupping her breasts, to look down and see his head between her…

Holy Christmas crackers! What was going on here?

Yanking her hand away, Adie stepped back and lifted her own glass to her lips, hoping he didn't notice. She didn't like feeling so out of control. Even in the old days, back when she'd used men and their attention as a distraction, she'd never experienced such an intense reaction. Back then, she'd been more concerned about what a man could do *for* her—mentally and emotionally as opposed to physically and financially—rather than what he did *to* her.

He stopped in front of a faceless gold mannequin wearing a tiny camisole and panties and cocked his head to the side. Tucking his jacket under his arm, he reached out and rubbed the silk between his thumb and finger.

"It's from one of the most exclusive and talented designers in the world. It's made from Lyon silk edged with Chantilly lace and comes in every color you can think of," Adie gabbled, her face heating. "Obviously she has other designs, if that's not your thing."

His lips quirked and those gorgeous eyes flashed with amusement. "It's not *my* thing at all. I'm more of a take-it-off than a try-it-on guy."

Adie smiled at his joke.

He cleared his throat and Adie forced her eyes to connect with his. Those eyes darkened, turned intense.

"Gorgeous," he stated, his eyes not moving off

hers. Adie wasn't sure whether he was referring to her or the lingerie or both. "I'd like to see it in its more natural setting…"

And she'd have no problem wearing it for him. She could easily imagine a huge bed, luxurious, sweet-smelling cotton sheets, a bottle of Moët in a silver ice bucket, fado music—expressive, passionate and melancholic—playing in the background.

And the late afternoon sun falling on the bed, turning his hair to burnished gold…

Adie quickly lowered her eyes, took a fortifying sip of whiskey and placed her glass on the table, grateful when he resumed his slow stroll down the tables, those light, intense eyes darting over her inventory. He picked up a hand-blown glass Christmas tree ornament, holding the gorgeous peacock design up to the light.

"It's mouth-blown and hand-painted. The crystals on its plumage are diamonds."

He didn't react but simply sipped his drink and looked down at the open box displaying Christmas crackers. "And these?"

Adie looked at his profile, wondering whether his wavy hair was as soft as it looked. She inhaled his woody, sunshiny smell. It took all her processing power to make sense of his question.

"Uh…handmade in the UK from eco-friendly luxury paper. They are tailor-made and the prizes can be anything you want. I had a client who bought each of his children a new car for Christmas and we inserted the car keys inside."

His lips quirked up in a half smile and Adie desperately wanted to know whether his mouth was as skilled as it was sexy. She really should have sex more often; this reaction was ridiculous. But, like relationships, random sexual encounters weren't her thing.

But she was seriously considering making this man the exception to her rule.

"I take it those kids didn't receive entry-level models."

Of course they didn't, her clients didn't understand the word *entry-level*. "Porsches and Lamborghinis."

He whistled and moved on.

"Are you in the market for something special?" Adie asked him, trying to judge whether he was a serious spender. His pants were quality, his shoes were expensive, but she couldn't tell if he was a billionaire or a millionaire or just rich. Unfortunately, if he was just rich, he wouldn't be able to afford what she was offering. Her products were aimed at the multimillionaire to billionaire section of the marketplace.

"Just looking."

Those words, she'd come to learn, were often code for I-like-it-but-I-can't-afford-it. Oh, well, he might not be good for business, but he was lovely to look at. Adie glanced down at her watch and noticed that it was past eleven and she still had a couple of hours of work ahead of her. She had a long day packed with meetings tomorrow and it was time to hustle Mr. Delicious along.

"No way!"

At his outburst, Adie's eyes flew to the object in his hand and she grinned. The centerpiece of the object was a 3.5-carat heart-shaped diamond, and more round diamonds studded the crocodile leather band.

"Is this a dog collar? For three hundred thousand?" he demanded, sounding and looking outraged.

"Gorgeous, isn't it?" Adie took the collar from his hand and examined the intricate work.

"How can anyone spend so much money on a dog? I'm mean, don't get me wrong, I love animals, but this amount of money?"

"My clients adore their animals," Adie explained.

She put down the dog collar and stacked the boxes of handmade chocolates and moved them to the side, giving her enough space to sit on the heavy table, her legs swinging. It felt so good to get off her aching feet. Picking up a sample dish of chocolates, she held it out to him.

He shook his head. "I rarely eat chocolate."

"You'll want to eat this," Adie assured him. "Have you ever tasted bacon and Mexican chili in chocolate?"

"That would be a no."

"It's rare, rather wonderful and…"

"Ridiculously expensive," he finished her sentence and smiled.

Adie snapped her fingers and pointed her index finger at him. "You're catching on." She watched as he slid the chocolate into his mouth, wishing it were her lips making contact with his, her tongue sliding against his. Adie wiggled in place and released a frustrated breath. Needing to do something with her hands, she picked up another chocolate truffle, looked at it and bit down on the bittersweet treat.

Gorgeous…rich, creamy and, hell, *hot*!

Adie chewed, swallowed and waved her hand in front of her mouth. She looked into his laughing, fog-colored eyes, and blushed. "Wasabi. Not what I was expecting…"

"Want some of mine?"

Adie looked at the half-eaten truffle in his fingers and wondered if he was going to feed her the rest of his chocolate. Suddenly desperate for some contact with him, any contact, she slowly nodded.

He seemed to hesitate, his eyes skimming her face. It was obvious to her that he was testing the waters, wanting to make sure he was interpreting her signals correctly.

He was.

His eyes held hers, fascinating and mysterious, as he placed the chocolate in his mouth and his hands on her knees. Heat skittered up her spine as he gently pushed her legs apart, stepping into the space he'd created. Adie held his eyes and her breath as he lowered his head…closer and closer until his lips were a whisper from hers. Unable to bear the suspense—she wanted his kiss more than she needed to breathe—she lifted her hands to his chest and placed her lips against his. Soft, hard, both at once and when his hot tongue on the seam of her lips cajoled her to open up, she willingly followed his lead. But instead of his tongue entering her mouth, she tasted bittersweet chocolate, a hint of chili, the rush of salty bacon. She moaned in delight.

Adie, wanting more—wanting everything—curled her hand around the back of his neck and held him in place, enjoying the chocolate-covered strokes of his tongue against hers, the way his fingertips pushed into the skin on her hips, his other hand cupping her jaw.

Adie heard him moan and then his hands were on her waist, hauling her closer so that the vee of her legs connected with his rigid erection, her feet curling around the backs of his knees.

Adie felt like she'd dived off a cliff into a warm, deep pool of delight. She ran her hands down his strong, muscled back, over his spectacular butt—and it felt as good as it looked. Her fingers danced over the backs of his thighs. She wanted this, she wanted more…to see him naked, to taste every inch of his hot, masculine skin.

It had been so very long…

He pulled back to drop kisses on her jaw, over her cheekbone, on her temple. His breathing was harsh in her ear and Adie reveled in the notion that he wanted her as much as she wanted him.

Had there ever been such a perfect kiss? Adie didn't think so…

Needing him, needing more, Adie gripped his jaw with one hand, seeking his mouth. Oblivious to where she was, she picked up his hand and placed it on her breast, groaning when the pad of his thumb brushed over her nipple. Tipping her head to the side, he changed the angle of the kiss, taking more, going deeper, silently demanding that she give him everything…

Adie pulled his shirt out of his pants and sighed into his mouth when her hands found hard muscles. She explored the bumps of his spine and when her hands moved over his sides and across his stomach, heading south, she felt his hand on hers, stopping her progress.

He stiffened, stopped kissing her, and after a moment lifted his mouth off hers.

He stared at her for the longest time, his eyes now steel gray with passion, his breathing ragged.

"You're beautiful," he muttered.

"Kiss me again," Adie begged, pleasure overwhelming her pride.

He shook his head. "If I do, I won't be able to stop."

Adie, knowing that this was wrong, that she was taking a massive risk, and not caring, lifted her shoulders in a small shrug. "So, don't stop."

A part of Adie hesitated, wondering what her real motivations were. Was she acting like this because it was that time of year? The season of doubts and regrets and over-thinking. During the festive season she always, always second guessed herself…

Was she making the right choices? Was she really happy with her life? What if this, what if that…

But no one had ever made her feel so much, so soon. It had been a long, long time since she'd used a man, and she'd never jumped into bed so quickly, but nobody had ever made her feel like this. She wanted more. She wanted one night of wild passion and if his kisses were a prelude to the main event, she was in for the treat of a lifetime.

She was a grown woman and she was allowed to explore her sexuality so, tonight, she wasn't going to second-guess herself, to wonder if she was falling back into old, destructive patterns. In the morning she could analyze her actions and deal with her regret, but she wasn't going to do that tonight.

Not with him.

"I have a room, upstairs," Adie whispered, her heart in her throat.

His thumb drifted over her bottom lip, tense and expectant. As he opened his mouth to speak, her phone jangled from across the room. Not interested in anything anyone else had to say, she stared at him, waiting for his answer. Why was he hesitating? Was he playing hard to get?

"I—" Her phone rang again and Adie, through

her lust, recognized the ring tone. It was Kate. If she didn't answer, her friend would keep calling. She was pain-in-the-ass persistent.

Adie pushed him back and jumped to the floor. "Sorry, if I don't answer, she'll keep calling."

He nodded and Adie brushed past him to walk over to her bag, yanking her phone out of the side pocket. Annoyed and frustrated, she scowled at the screen and jabbed the answer button.

"What?"

"I just realized that I left you to pack up. I'm on my way back to help you…"

Seriously? Nooooo!

"I don't like you being on your own with so many valuable items. I mean, the security there is good, but anyone could con his way in…"

Adie's eyes darted across the room to where he stood, hands in his pockets, pulling the fabric of his pants against his still-hard erection. Who was he and what was he really doing here? As blood returned to her brain, Kate's words sank in and Adie bit her lip, her eyes flying over the table. Had he kissed her to distract her, so he could slip something valuable into his pocket? The dog collar was too big but the diamond-encrusted bottle stoppers and the gold memory sticks were easily hidden.

And had she really invited him up to her room? Would she have walked away with him without securing the room? Possibly.

Probably.

Oh, God…what the hell was wrong with her? He was a stranger and she'd been about to risk her body and her safety and her business? She was acting like she had when she was a young adult, impulsively and without thought, looking for attention, a distraction.

She refused to go back there, go back to that person she'd been. She'd worked too hard to jeopardize everything she'd work so hard to achieve, to become the person she was.

No man, no matter how attracted she was to him, was worth her backsliding even an inch.

Adie disconnected her call with Kate and folded her arms across her chest, forcing herself to meet his eyes. Passion had fled and his gaze was now concrete gray and hard.

"I see the moment has passed and your offer has been withdrawn."

Adie bit her bottom lip. She jerked her head toward the door. "I think I got a bit carried away," she said, her voice low. "If you'll excuse me, I have work to do."

He walked over and stopped an inch from her. Adie refused to move—her pride was back—and she kept her folded arms as a barrier against him coming any closer.

She stiffened as he dropped a kiss on the corner of her mouth. "Don't hurt yourself counting stock, I didn't steal anything." He dropped another kiss on her cheekbone and then her temple. "Thanks for the chocolate. And the drink."

"It was nice meeting you." He gave her a sexy smirk but Adie noticed his smile didn't soften his eyes. "But kissing you was better."

Adie said nothing as he turned away. She watched him walk to the door, biting down on her bottom lip to keep herself from calling him back, from begging him to take her up to her room and show her how good sex could be.

Because she knew with him it would be too bloody fantastic.

Christmas was a pain in the ass, Hunter Sheridan decided, leaning back in his chair and placing his feet on the corner of his desk.

After Thanksgiving, productivity went down, laziness went up and it felt like every one of his employees was distracted by thinking about, planning for and chatting over holiday festivities.

If Hunter had his way, the entire holiday would be canceled. But, while Christmas meant less than nothing to him, there were people out there obsessed with the holiday and who were, judging by what he'd seen last night, prepared to spend a lot of money celebrating.

Three hundred thousand for a dog collar? Wow.

Hunt leaned back in his chair and dug his fingers into his eye sockets, reluctantly admitting that dog collars and wine stoppers and bittersweet chocolate weren't foremost on his mind.

Adie Ashby-Tate was.

Oh, he'd known who she was the moment he stepped into the ballroom of the Grantham-Forrester. He instantly recognized her from Kate's incessant social media posts. And who else but the owner of the company would be the last to leave?

With her shaggy, short espresso-colored curls cut close to her head and her delicate features, she reminded him of a young Audrey Hepburn. Her skin was a deep shade of cream, and her eyes...

He ran his hand through his hair and blew out a long stream of air. Those eyes... Jesus, they were gorgeous. Against her luminous skin, they were the color of dark coffee beans tipped onto winter snow.

Her body, slim but curvy, had been a revelation and she'd fit him perfectly, as if she were a puzzle piece he hadn't known he was missing.

Puzzle piece, luminous skin, the action in his pants... How old was he, thirty-five or fifteen?

Hunt rubbed his hand over his jaw. He'd been immediately attracted to her looks, but catching her at the end of her event, he'd seen the woman beneath the salesperson, a woman more down-to-earth than he'd expected for someone completely immersed in their world, *his* world.

It was a place laced with over-the-top opulence, fantastic service and unforgettable experiences. It was a world of excess and bling, instant gratification, pride and arrogance. According to his online research, her father was a British lord, her mother an American tobacco heiress and she was their only child. Adie's mother was a former famous model, her father was once—before inheriting a fortune from his parents—a professional polo player. These days, her father didn't seem to do much of anything, choosing to hop from superyacht to superyacht, mansion to mansion in the pursuit of pleasure, accompanied by a variety of young, busty women.

Their daughter was very much a product of that rich, aristocratic world. Adie's dress, a shorty frothy number, had been designer, and fat diamond studs had glinted in her pretty earlobes. Her perfume was expensive and her accent was upper-class British, thoroughly classy. She was the real deal, a proper aristocrat and, although he hadn't seen her working the room, Hunt knew she'd done it with grace and charm.

He should've introduced himself, that much was obvious, but if he had, he wouldn't have gotten to kiss her, hold her slim body against his, feel her sleek curves under his shaky fingers. He'd been surprised at her offer to go upstairs—because she hadn't seemed the type—but he'd wanted to accept her unexpected offer, because, hell, that kiss blew his socks off.

Knowing that she needed to know who she was going to bed with—a potential client, one of the most influential business people in the city, according to Kate—he'd been about to introduce himself when her damn phone rang.

He'd watched as a frisson of fear and wariness

replaced lust in her eyes and he'd seen his chance slipping away.

By the time she'd finished her conversation, it was obvious she was having second thoughts about what she'd proposed. So, he'd kissed her goodbye, knowing he'd see her again in less than eighteen hours.

And that they'd soon be picking up where they'd left off.

Hunt massaged the tight knot in his right trapezius muscle, thinking that he had work to do, lots of it. But, because he was acting like an adolescent, he couldn't stop thinking about Adie's sweet and sensuous kiss. It had been the sexiest of his life and, had they gotten to the really good stuff, Hunt thought there would have been a good chance of them setting the hotel on fire.

It had been that hot.

He couldn't remember when last, if ever, he'd had that same take-her-to-the-floor reaction to a woman. He'd been busy lately and hadn't slept with anyone but Griselda for more than a year, not because he was committed to her or their arrangement—he wasn't—but because he'd been too busy to bother.

Right now, he'd ditch everything...

EVERY.

THING.

...to take Adie Ashby-Tate to bed.

Hunt released a frustrated growl, annoyed that he couldn't move his focus and concentration onto anything other than a gorgeous woman with big brown eyes and a pixie face.

This wasn't who he was, wasn't what he did. He was never distracted by women and he never allowed them to affect his productivity. Work was all that was important.

He had several companies to run, a legacy to create, goals to reach. People—women, friends, acquaintances—sucked up time when he could be working. But here he was, completely distracted.

God.

Help.

Him.

Hunt heard the door to his office open and looked up as his long-time assistant approached his desk, staring down at his tablet. "So, Griselda is off the list of people for whom I must purchase a Christmas gift? Is that correct?"

Very. "Yep."

Hunt noticed the curiosity in Duncan's eyes, but didn't explain that he'd broken off his two-year— Fling? Liaison? Affair?—with Griselda a few days earlier when she'd asked him to consider co-raising a child with her. His "hell no" had been rather emphatic and his ending of their fling/liaison/affair had been the vehement exclamation point on that subject.

Honestly, people exhausted him.

He'd thought he'd hit the jackpot with Griselda. Thanks to his bouncing between foster families and group homes as a kid, his short but drama-filled marriage, and his best friend and business partner's death, he'd deliberately chosen a woman who made no demands, financial or emotional. And Gris never had. Until the other day when she'd asked him to father her child.

And all thoughts of his ex faded on meeting Adie last night…

Duncan pursed his lips. "Well, not buying Griselda an expensive piece of art or jewelry should save you a pretty penny."

Hunt swallowed his smile and hoped his expression remained inscrutable. Even after so many years as his PA, Duncan still acted as if Hunt were on the knife-edge of slipping into debt. Since he had enough money for a hundred lifetimes, even if he chose never to work another day in his life, Duncan's penny-pinching and cost-cutting attitude was a constant source of amusement.

Leaning back in his chair, Hunt looked up and noticed a deeper worry in Duncan's eyes, something more intense than the cost of gifts. Duncan was almost as stoic and implacable as Hunt so seeing his stressed face was a surprise.

"Everything okay?" Hunt asked, sitting up and leaning forward.

Duncan gripped the back of the visitor's chair and shook his head. "I just got an email… Uh, my first partner, the man I thought I was going to marry, is in the hospital after suffering from what they are calling a brain episode. For some reason, and although we haven't been together for more than fifteen years, he designated me to make any medical decisions if he's incapacitated. And, he's incapacitated."

Hunt heard the surprised confusion, and the intense fear, in Duncan's voice. "I'm sorry."

Duncan's head bobbed up and down in a terse acknowledgment of Hunt's sympathy. "I know it's not a good time for me to take a leave of absence, there's so much that needs doing concerning your foundation's annual fundraiser."

Honestly, Hunt had mostly forgotten about the yearly Christmas fundraiser. This year they were trying something new—an urban treasure hunt race. All the funds raised would go to support the Williams-Sheridan Foundation, named in honor of his and best friend, Steve's friendship.

Duncan quietly and efficiently organized everything, and Hunt's involvement was to show up at the cocktail party and hand out prizes to the winning teams.

Duncan also purchased Christmas gifts for Hunt's biggest clients, his favorite suppliers, for the sports players who acted as his brand ambassadors. As his right-hand man, Duncan made Hunt's life run smoothly. Duncan not only managed his office with aplomb, he also booked theater tickets, made reservations, dealt with Hunt's housekeepers and interior designers and made suggestions for and booked Hunt's infrequent holiday breaks.

And Duncan made Christmas bearable by shielding Hunt from the chaos of the season. But Duncan needed personal time and Hunt had to put his assistant's needs first. He'd survive Christmas…

Maybe.

"Call Jeff and tell him to file a flight plan and leave as soon as you can."

Gratitude at the casual offer to use his private jet flashed across Duncan's face. "I can book a commercial flight, it will be so much cheaper…" Duncan protested.

And jam-packed and stressful while Hunt's plane and pilot were just sitting there, doing nothing. "Use my plane, Duncan," Hunt told him, using his don't-argue-with-me voice.

Duncan nodded his thanks. "Concerning work, I'm pretty sure I'll be just sitting around at the hospital so I can still be productive. I'll have my laptop and phone with me."

Hunt stood up and walked around the desk to briefly lay his hand on Duncan's shoulder. "Work if you want to, Duncan, but not because you have to. Be with your friend."

Because, God knew, Hunt would do anything for a couple more hours, days, with Steve.

Duncan looked down, sighed and then he straightened his spine and blinked back the sheen of moisture in his eyes. "Thank you, Hunter, I appreciate it."

Duncan picked up a couple of folders, straightened them and placed them on the corner of Hunt's desk. He picked up a couple of pens and dusted some used staples off Hunt's desk into his hand. Hunter smiled at his assistant's fussing.

"Kate and Adie Ashby-Tate will be with you in five minutes."

Hunt was looking forward to seeing Steve's twin Kate. It had been a while, although she had called earlier in the week to ask him to attend the Christmas market last night.

"I'll finish up a few things here, but I'll be in touch, as soon as I can, with a plan on how I'm going to manage my duties regarding your Christmas schedule, your functions and the treasure hunt race."

God, Hunt hoped he would. He was lost without Duncan.

Seeing the time, Hunter stood up and buttoned his suit jacket, smoothing down his designer tie. Hunter walked over to his massive floor-to-ceiling window overlooking Central Park and scowled at the dark gray clouds. Snow was predicted for that evening, just a light dusting, but that wouldn't stop Hunt from his daily run around the park. Keeping fit kept him sane and he needed to spend a little time each day outside. If he didn't, he felt like the walls of his office and apartment were closing in on him, pulling to the surface memories of being locked up in group houses.

After his meeting with Kate and Adie, he'd walk toward the park and back. That would do him until he could pull on his exercise gear. Hunter turned at the brief knock on his door and saw Duncan pushing it open.

"Your four-thirty is here, Hunter."

Hunter looked at the slim woman walking into his office, immediately taking in her tousled brown hair and bright red, sensuous mouth.

There she was…

And it terrified Hunter to realize that he'd missed this woman he didn't know.

Two

Stepping into an enormous light-filled office—thanks to the floor-to-ceiling windows framing a helluva view of Central Park—Adie pulled a professional, happy-to-meet-you smile onto her face. This meeting was important. Hunter Sheridan was Kate's friend, her hotshot influencer and the one Adie needed to snag if she had any chance of making fast inroads into the crème de la crème of Manhattan society.

Kate, as she'd explained to Adie, didn't understand why Hunter Sheridan wielded so much influence, but maybe it was, per Kate, because he didn't give a damn what society thought about him or whether they accepted him or not. Hunt, Kate said with a smile, was a true individual, and while he could be charming if he tried, he could also be rude, demanding and impatient.

He was a hard man…

Adie, laying eyes on the man standing near the window knew just how very hard this man could be.

Stopping suddenly, her eyes clashed with his. She understood, somehow, that he'd known exactly who she was last night…

While she hadn't known anything about him at all.

She'd thought him to be anyone other than Manhattan's Most Magnificent. Though today he did look the part, Adie reluctantly conceded.

He was a natural clotheshorse and she loved his black Italian designer suit. His shirt was white, his tie silver and, if she'd had any doubt about his wealth last night, she had none this morning. He looked like what he obviously was—megarich and powerful.

And she'd asked him, without knowing his name, to come upstairs with her, to see her naked.

God, she couldn't be more humiliated if she'd walked through Knightsbridge naked with her hypercritical mother pointing out all her flaws to pedestrians passing by.

Adie had spent many hours since their encounter cursing him, but mostly cursing herself. Falling into a man's arms wasn't what she did, not anymore at least. In her teens and twenties, she'd been addicted to attention, throwing herself into the arms of any man who would catch her. She'd fall in love easily and completely, convinced that this guy would be the one to give her what she so desperately craved: love, time, attention, a family.

Most of the guys ran, scared by her intensity. But a few stuck and because she was completely messed up, when they offered to take the relationship to the next level—handing her an "I love you," a "let's move in together" or even a "will you marry me?"—she was the one who galloped away.

Because the thing she wanted the most also terrified her to death.

And really, she now knew that it was better to be alone than to be rejected.

Because nothing lasted forever.

Five years ago, soon after turning twenty-five, she'd wised up and realized that her behavior was destructive and demeaning. After a lot of self-reflection, she accepted the fact that she constantly sought attention because she'd never received any from her parents as a child. She accepted the fact that she used guys and relationships as a distraction to fill the holes in her heart. After years of chasing love, she'd decided that she no longer wanted it. She needed to learn to be happy on her own.

By keeping busy and living an over-full life, she'd become strong and independent, totally career focused and committed to providing her clients with six-star service. She never allowed any romantic relationships to develop, terrified she'd revert back to being that demanding, clingy woman she'd been.

And sex was a vague memory.

But Christmas was always a bad time of year for her, and Adie knew the stress of the holiday season triggered sadness and depression in lots of people. She wasn't immune. As the festive season rolled around, and images of perfect people, families and situations bombarded her, she was reminded of her ugly childhood and neglectful parents. Seeing Kate with her mom last night at the Christmas market had rubbed salt into that particular wound...

It was obvious that mother and daughter took great delight in each other and adored being in each other's company. Rachel, despite being a successful attorney, took her role as a mother very seriously. Her kids, as Kate told Adie, were the reason Rachel's sun rose every morning. Losing her twin brother, Steve, had devastated Kate, but Rachel was the one who took a year off work, who'd been unable to function for months after Steve's death.

Adie had no doubt that should something happen to her, her mom would hold a very tasteful funeral and cry prettily. Lady Vivien Ashby-Tate had the emotional depth of a puddle and after a week, she'd become bored with playing the mourning mommy.

Adie pushed her hand through her short-cropped hair, wishing she could chide herself for being harsh. But the reality was that her mom didn't love her, never had, and Adie was a burden her parents wished they'd never been saddled with.

Seeing Kate and Rachel together had made all

those old feelings of neglect and need float to the surface. She'd berated herself for not being in a relationship, for not pursuing her dream of having a family. She'd felt herself slipping back into neediness. And that was before the sexiest man she'd ever laid eyes on walked through the door.

She was mostly happy. For most of the year, she was content with being single and having a kick-ass career. But as December edged closer, the Christmas blues made their arrival and she routinely started to question what she wanted, what she needed.

Every year, the fight to stay the independent, strong woman she was became harder.

All she could do was distract herself, to run herself ragged in order not to think. Christmas was her busiest time so keeping up with her clients' last-minute requests kept her to-do list full. For the past couple of years, she'd also fitted in as many hours as she could as a volunteer. Last year, she'd helped organize a London-wide food drive for homeless people. The year before, she was the stage manager for a local pantomime production.

This year her distraction of choice was trying to establish a new business in New York.

It was not giving in to more kisses from Hunter Sheridan.

"Kate, Adie."

Adie felt the confused look Kate sent her way, but she couldn't drop her eyes from Hunter's compelling face. She'd kissed those lips, had her hands on the bare skin of his stomach, felt his erection pressing against her…

Please, world, open up a portal and drop me into it.

"Have you two met?" Kate demanded, throwing her bag onto the couch in the corner of Hunt's office.

Hunt walked, gracefully for a man of his size, over to the couch, picked up Kate's Birkin tote, and pushed it into her arms. "We need a minute, Kate. Maybe more than a minute. Go talk to Duncan, he needs someone right now."

Kate frowned at him. "But we have a meeting…"

"Katherine. Go."

Kate's frown deepened at the command in Hunter's voice and turned her eyes in Adie's direction. Adie, convinced she was as red as a beetroot, gave her friend a quick nod. Kate didn't need to be here while Adie sorted out this mess. She was embarrassed enough.

"Give us ten, Katie," Adie said, finding her voice.

Kate threw up her hands, obviously exasperated. "Okay, then."

Adie waited until the door closed behind Kate before making eye contact with Hunt again. "You're Hunter Sheridan."

Hunt's mouth twitched at her pronouncement and Adie closed her eyes, cursing her stupid statement. Who else would he be?

Adie tried again. "So, this is awkward…"

Hunt folded his arms across his chest, revealing the face of his watch. Adie, because it was her job, instantly recognized the timepiece. It was one of only ten from a renowned Swiss maker who was so in demand there was a decade-long waiting list. If she'd seen that watch last night, she would've instantly placed him in her can-afford-anything-anywhere box. Him being a potential client might've made her act with more propriety but she couldn't swear to it.

The wretched man was that compelling.

"Last night I thought you were someone else…" It was a weak explanation but the only one she had.

Amusement flashed in his eyes. "Who?"

"Well, not *you*, obviously," Adie crossly replied. "If I knew you were Hunt Sheridan, I would never have suggested…"

"Taking me upstairs?" Hunt lifted his thick eyebrows. "Really? How…novel. Normally, it's the other way around."

Adie looked at his mouth, remembered how skilled he was at kissing her and calculated the distance between them. A couple of steps and she'd be in his arms…

No, she wouldn't allow him to be her Christmas distraction, her festive fling… She didn't play those games anymore. He wasn't the way to deal with her feelings of abandonment, of being unloved and neglected. He wouldn't help her forget about cold Christmases spent with strangers who ignored her or her grandmother who detested her. That was when she was young. After she turned ten, it was normal for her to spend most of the festive season alone.

Christmas had never been a fun time of year.

Hunter couldn't change that.

But he *could* make or break her Manhattan business.

She had to keep him at arm's length…

Adie stared at a point behind his shoulder and forced out her apology. "I do apologize. I wasn't very professional last night."

"No, you weren't," Hunt agreed, his tone measured and calm. "You weren't wearing any shoes— you have pretty toes by the way. You tossed back superb whiskey like it was juice, fed me chocolate and invited me into your bed."

Yeah, she remembered. She'd been there.

"I'll completely understand if you don't want to proceed with this meeting," Adie said, her words stiff.

Hunt had the temerity to flash a megawatt grin. "No, you're here and I'll listen to your pitch. But…"

Adie held her breath as he walked across the room to stand in front of her, hands in his pockets, completely at ease. He stared down at her, his eyes an enigmatic color between gray and blue. "But, at some time in the future, rain or shine, hail or hellfire, we will pick up where we left off last night."

Adie saw the heated desire in his eyes and knew he was thinking of how he'd held her in his arms, his hand on her breast, his other hand under her skirt, down the back of her panties. He'd rocketed her from zero to a hundred in seconds and, had Kate not called her last night, this meeting would be a hundred times more awkward.

And it was plenty awkward already. Mostly because she still really, desperately, wanted to strip him naked and do wicked, wicked things to him.

Without giving her a chance to respond, Hunt sidestepped to the right and walked over to the door, yanking it open. "Kate, come back in, we've got work to do."

Adie stared at his broad back, bemused, confused and—dammit—wholly turned on.

Thank God Adie'd done this pitch a hundred times before and could recite the words by rote. There was nothing too big, too costly or too complicated for her to fulfill. She touched on what she could offer him as a concierge in terms of travel—luxury villas and upmarket hotel suites, adventure holidays and reservations at the best restaurants wherever in the world he happened to be.

Hunt's face remained impassive and, worse, unimpressed. She mentioned backstage passes to sold-out music and culture events. He finally showed a hint of interest when she mentioned the best box seats at sports stadiums. The purchasing of personalized gifts for employees, friends and family raised another flicker of interest and she ended by reassuring him that, by employing Treasures and Tasks, he'd enjoy white-glove service in every aspect of his life.

Hunt picked up her glossy brochure and thumbed

through it. Adie gently bit the inside of her lip, wishing she could read him. She'd never met anyone with such a poker face. This wasn't the man she'd met last night, the one with passion in his eyes. No, this Hunt was all business. Adie thought they might be wasting their time. He didn't seem impressed by anything she'd said.

She knew that some people called her a glorified personal assistant, but she didn't care. She loved arranging personal experiences, like over-the-top wedding proposals and anniversary dinners, private meals cooked by fabulous chefs, wine tastings in galleries and private viewings of museums and art galleries by world-renowned curators. She loved facilitating experiences that would create lifelong memories…

But, to be honest, buying another diamond bracelet or superbike for a spoiled child didn't excite her.

Maybe it was because her parents thought luxury gifts were an adequate substitute for their time and affection. Instead of the Victorian mini-mansion playhouse she'd received at eight and the pony she was given at ten, she would've far preferred for them to read her a story, drive her to school or—novel idea—live in the same house with her.

Or at the very least, be there on Christmas morning.

Hunt pulled a writing pad toward him, picked up a fountain pen and dashed words across the page. After ripping off the sheet and passing it to her, Hunt leaned back in his chair and linked his fingers over his flat stomach. Adie looked down at the list he'd handed her and quickly read through the bullet points. They ranged from buying Christmas gifts to organizing a couple of cocktail parties, decorating his apartment and booking a surfing holiday in Jeffrey's Bay sometime in the New Year.

The last item on the list was the one that intrigued her the most: to help with the final arrangements for his foundation's urban treasure hunt race… Now, that sounded interesting.

Adie placed the paper on his desk and crossed her legs. Hoping her expression matched his inscrutable one, she lifted one eyebrow, waiting for an explanation.

"Duncan takes care of most of what you provide. And he does his job exceptionally well."

She wouldn't be getting any business from him, Adie thought. Why would he pay her when he had his own personal concierge on staff? Now all she could hope for was that his fondness for Kate would prompt him to mention Treasures and Tasks to his rich friends. If Adie didn't sign up some new clients on retainer, she couldn't justify the costs of setting up a satellite branch in Manhattan.

Hunt continued, "However, Duncan is leaving shortly for a family emergency. I doubt he'll be back before Christmas and while he says he's going to carry on working, I don't want him to feel torn between his duty to someone he loves and his job." Hunt held Adie's eyes and she caught the flash of emotion in his expression, there and gone too fast for her to discern what he was feeling. He leaned forward and tapped the paper she'd placed on the desk. "I'm prepared to hire you to fill in for him. I presume you can handle all of this?"

Adie internally scoffed. Was he kidding? Compared to arranging a Michelin chef to cook in an igloo so her clients could have dinner under the northern lights, this was child's play.

"We can," Adie replied, picking up the list again. She frowned at the last item. "Can you give me a little more detail about the urban treasure hunt race?"

"It's my foundation's primary fundraising event of the year. Teams of two—one a professional sportsperson and one an underprivileged teen from one of the sports programs the foundation runs—race through lower Manhattan, looking for clues. The sports stars raise money for the foundation by asking people they know to pledge an amount for every leg completed. We receive a lot of corporate donations, as well."

"And when is it?"

Hunt grimaced. "This coming weekend. The hunt happens on Saturday, culminating in a cocktail party where we give out prizes."

"That sounds like so much fun," Kate said, smiling. "And Duncan arranged it all himself?"

Hunt returned Kate's smile and it was pure affection. "Duncan handled the entrants and matching the sports stars with the kids. There's a company that handles all the race details, they set up the route and place people along the way who hand out clues. The contestants just run around Manhattan, searching for clues and the first team to arrive at the designated endpoint earns money toward the teen's college fund. The professional teammate wins triple matching funds from the foundation for the money they've raised. Everyone wins prizes at the evening event, as well." Hunt shrugged. "Duncan will know the details."

Adie's mind was running at warp speed. "What still needs to be done regarding the race?"

Hunt looked at her. "I know there are some outstanding issues. I'll ask Duncan to send you the list of what hasn't been confirmed. Expect it sometime later this evening."

"Is Duncan still on the premises?" Adie asked Hunter.

He looked at his watch and nodded. "My driver will be collecting him in five minutes to take him to the airport. He's flying out shortly."

"On your Gulfstream?" Kate asked him.

Hunt nodded. "Yeah."

Adie turned in her seat to face Kate and handed her Hunt's list. "Can you go with Duncan to the airport and get all the information you can about how far he's got with regard to the various bullet points on this list? We might have to call him later, but I'd prefer not to disturb him after he's gone unless we really have to."

"I've already asked him to email you the file on the urban treasure hunt," Hunt interjected.

"Okay, good. Then go through all these other bullet points. I bet there are at least twenty things not on this list. Get those too."

Kate nodded and stood up. "I'm on it."

Adie smiled up at her. "Thanks, honey. I'll see you back at your place later, there are just a couple of points I need to iron out with Mr. Sheridan."

Kate sent her an uncertain look at the formal use of Hunt's name, but Adie gave the tiniest of head shakes and Kate nodded. After walking around the desk, she dropped a kiss on Hunt's cheek and sauntered from the room, moving easily on her spiky heels.

Hunt watched Kate leave and when the door closed behind her, he spoke again. "I think Kate is going to like working as a private concierge. It will suit her vibrant personality."

It wasn't what Adie had expected him to say. "I think it will too, but we need to pick up some clients before I can afford to employ her on a long-term basis. Kate, with her connections, will be expensive."

Hunt pushed his chair back and stood up, walking over to the state-of-the-art coffee machine in the corner of his large office. He offered her a cup and when Adie declined, he fixed himself a cup of coffee—unsweetened and black—and carried it over to the large window, leaning his shoulder into the glass.

Adie followed him and echoed his stance, folding her arms across her chest.

"I need help, at least until Duncan comes back." Hunt sipped from his cup, his gray eyes looking at her over the rim. "How does it work and how much do you cost?"

Adie ran over the financial implications, gave him a ballpark figure, and suggested that she send over a quote and a contract later.

"Well, it's not like I have much of a choice. Duncan's unavailable and I don't want to organize cocktail parties and decorate trees and go shopping."

"Well, Kate and I are happy to take care of all that for you," Adie told him, trying to sound brisk.

"Good." Hunt placed his cup on the bookcase nearby and turned to face her, moving closer until she could feel the heat radiating off him. He smelled so good, of soap and man and something expensive but understated. She wanted to bury her face in his neck and just inhale…

He can't be your Christmas caper, Adie. You've got enough on your plate without indulging in a festive fling.

And, as she'd reminded herself earlier, distracting herself by jumping into the arms of a man wasn't something she did anymore. It had been years since she'd been tempted to engage in that sort of behavior—

Hunt trailed his fingers over her cheek. "I haven't stopped thinking about kissing you. You've been on my mind all day."

—but, damn, Sheridan was temptation personified. Adie turned her cheek into his open palm.

"I don't sleep with my clients, Hunt." Was she informing him or reminding herself?

Both.

"That's sensible," Hunt said, bending down to nibble his way up her jaw. Adie tipped her chin up and to the side to give him better access.

From a place far away, sensible Adie spoke. "Seriously, Hunt, I don't sleep with my clients." Even back in the day, sleeping with a guy was a very big deal and most of her relationships imploded long before they got to that point.

"Haven't signed the contract yet…" Hunt muttered.

"But you will."

"Later," Hunt insisted, his lips moving over hers. Adie, knowing she should resist him, opened her mouth anyway, and when his tongue touched hers, she groaned. This was better, if at all possible, than last night. He seemed harder, tougher, sexier and she wanted him with every atom pulsing in her body.

And because she'd never felt this way, with anyone, ever, Adie pulled out of his arms and stepped back, her hands raised in a "back off" gesture. Whatever was zinging between them felt too intense, too powerful. He was a tsunami of soul-and-breath-and-thought-stealing lust.

Hunt, thank God, got the message, and instead of reaching for her, jammed his hands in his pockets.

Adie, having noticed the very impressive erection tenting his pants, kept her eyes on his face. Yeah, the implacable distant businessman was gone, and a frustrated man stood in front of her. But Adie knew, soul-deep, that he wouldn't push her down a road she wasn't one hundred percent happy to walk.

"This isn't a good idea, Hunter."

"You thought it was an excellent idea last night," Hunt pointed out.

"I didn't know who you were last night and our mutual attraction caught me off guard," Adie replied. Off guard was an understatement, but he didn't need to know that.

"I don't date," Adie blurted out, needing to end this conversation.

Hunt barely reacted. "Neither do I."

That wasn't the reply she'd been expecting. "Why not?"

"I enjoy uncomplicated, no-strings-attached sex." It was an answer, but not to the question she'd asked.

With Hunter Sheridan, nothing was uncomplicated. Not their mutual desire, nor her desperate need to get her hands on him nor the flustered way he made her feel. Oh, she'd very much enjoy what he'd teach her sexually, but a roll around a big bed with him wasn't worth sacrificing the hard work she'd done to get to this point.

She no longer needed to chase attention, to look for validation in all the wrong places.

But what if she just wanted sex from him, her

inner voice wheedled. Well, tough. It was Christmas and because the season made her feel emotional and vulnerable, she couldn't take the chance.

No, it was better not to take any risks.

Hunt swiped his thumb over her bottom lip before dropping his hand to his side. "I'm not going to push you, Adie. But anytime you want to change your mind, you know where to find me."

Adie straightened her shoulders and her spine. "I'm not going to change my mind."

Well, she'd *try* not to.

Hunt smiled his devastatingly sexy half smile, half smirk. "Oh, I think you will. Hopefully sooner rather than later."

Adie's mouth fell open at his arrogance, but before she could form the words to slap down his ego, he looked at his watch. "I need to get back to work. Send me your quote and the contract and I'll look it over."

Adie blinked, dizzy from his rapid change of subject. "Okay."

Hunt walked over to his desk and slid a card from a silver box on his desk. Flipping it over, he scribbled on the back before handing it to her. "That's my private phone number, you can reach me on it anytime, anywhere. Feel free to use it."

Adie didn't need him to draw her a picture. "I won't."

"Yeah, I think you will," Hunt replied, amused. "And I expect to see you here, twice a day, once in the morning and again in the evening, to keep me updated."

Adie glared at him. "I could just send you an email!"

Hunt picked up her bag, gestured for her to walk over to the door. He opened it and dropped her bag over her shoulder. "Yeah, you could, but that wouldn't be any fun."

"I didn't think you were the fun type," Adie told him, feeling cross and outmaneuvered.

"I'm not, but I'll make an exception for you." Hunt bent down and dropped a kiss on the corner of her mouth. "See you back here at nine tomorrow morning. Unless..."

"Unless what?"

He nodded to the card in her hand. "Unless you call me between now and then."

Adie, not knowing how to respond or what else to do, stomped away.

Three

After a few days in Manhattan, and at Kate's insistence, Adie had moved into the guest room of Kate's Chelsea apartment.

She was mostly house trained, Kate laughingly informed her when making the offer, but she wasn't great at mornings. She'd been telling the truth. Adie, dressed to make her way to the Upper East Side and Hunt's building, shook her head at Kate's bedhead and dopey eyes.

Knowing that she needed some answers from her friend, Adie hastily poured Kate a cup of coffee, fixed it the way she liked it and shoved her into a seat at the small table in the kitchen. Then Adie pushed the cup into Kate's hands, hoping her return to reality wouldn't take too long.

The first sip did nothing, neither did the second. Kate's eyes remained foggy.

Adie picked up her tub of yogurt. "Come on, Williams, I need to go, and I need you to wake up and focus."

Kate lifted up a finger and took another few sips of her coffee. When she stood up to refill her cup, Adie knew she was on her way back to the land of the living.

Picking up her tablet, Adie opened the list she was working on and fired a couple of questions at Kate. Jotting down her responses with her stylus, she nodded. She asked Kate whether she'd contacted caterers for Hunt's annual Christmas cocktail party and received a laconic reply.

"So what's going on between you and Hunt?" Kate asked, looking at Adie over the rim of her cup.

"Nothing," Adie replied, turning around to throw her plastic yogurt container in the trash. And that was the truth. Nothing was happening and nothing was going to happen between her and Hunt. No Christmas, or any other type of, flings for her.

"Pfft! I don't believe you."

"Why wouldn't you?"

"We've had a couple of meetings with Hunt and the room feels ten degrees hotter whenever you are together and the chemistry between you crackles," Kate said, lifting her feet to rest her heels on the edge of her seat.

"Yeah, we're attracted to each other, but nothing is going to happen." She'd give Kate that much.

"Why not?" Kate demanded. "Is it because of Griselda?"

Who? Adie shook her head, confused. "Who is Griselda?"

Kate pulled a face, looking uneasy. "Uh…she's well, uh… I don't know how to describe her."

"Try," Adie snapped. When Kate didn't reply, she repeated the question, pushing the words through gritted teeth. Okay, she was totally overreacting here. She had no right to be jealous. She and Hunt had only shared a couple of kisses and he wanted to sleep with her…

But if he had a girlfriend, she'd be not only furious with him, but she'd be disappointed in him too. Her parents openly flaunted their affairs and, as a result, Adie deeply respected commitment and fidelity. If she did indulge in flings, affairs or brief relationships, men involved in relationships would be strictly off-limits.

And her questions didn't mean she was going to have a fling with Hunter Sheridan! But there was nothing wrong in gathering intelligence…

"Is she his girlfriend? Partner? Significant other?" Adie demanded, conscious of a tiny ache in her heart. No, she refused to feel disappointed or hurt. She'd met Hunt Sheridan a few days ago; she had no right to feel possessive…

They'd kissed, twice. She was totally over-reacting. Totally.

Kate wrinkled her nose. "Nah…"

"You don't sound convinced," Adie stated, folding her arms against her chest.

"I don't know how to describe what they are, Ades, and no, I'm not avoiding the question."

Adie glared at her, picked up her tablet and accessed the internet. She typed "Hunt Sheridan + girlfriend" into the search bar and cursed when her screen filled with dozens of results. Adie opened a popular online magazine and felt her heart sink at the photographs of Hunt at a prestigious gala, his strong arm around an exquisite woman's tiny waist.

As a child, Adie desperately wanted to be taller, blonder—more of a Cinderella than a Cinders. Griselda was exactly who Adie wanted to be when she grew up. Like Adie's mother, Vivien, Griselda was a tall, skinny, elegant, cool blonde who owned her own string of dance studios. She'd been a prima ballerina before injury cut her career short, and she and Hunt, according to the website, had been an item for two or so years.

Adie lifted her head to look at Kate. "The press calls her his girlfriend."

Kate waved her comment away. "Hunt doesn't. As far as I know, their relationship is…undefined." Kate shoved her hand into her hair, obviously uncomfortable. "Just ask Hunt if you want to know."

"I'm not interested."

Kate laughed at her ludicrous statement. "Of course you are, you're nuts about him!"

"Am not."

Kate's smile grew wider. "Oh, honey, you can lie to yourself but not me." Kate ran her finger up and down her coffee mug, her expression turning serious.

"I can't talk about her, Adie. I won't talk about her and Hunt's relationship. Just like I wouldn't talk to Hunt about your relationships."

Adie had to appreciate Kate's loyalty and her disinclination to gossip.

"Of course, you'd have to have a love life for me to talk about it," Kate pointed out.

Adie stuck out her tongue at her friend. It was a childish gesture, but effective.

Kate's grin slowly faded. "If you really want to know, ask Hunt."

"Kate!" Adie wheedled, pride taking a beating from her curiosity. "Don't leave me hanging, tell me about Grisella."

"Griselda," Kate corrected her, "and no, I won't. Besides, you said there wasn't anything happening between you and him so why do you care?"

Kate walked away, leaving her words hanging in the air. Adie resisted the impulse to wrestle her to the ground and beat the information out of her.

And Kate, damn her, was right. Adie had no intention of having any type of fling, Christmas or otherwise, with Hunter and she didn't care that he had a girlfriend. Market research in Manhattan was this year's distraction of choice and so far, it was doing a pretty crap job.

She had to up her game. Immediately.

Hunt missed his early morning meeting with Adie as he'd flown to Chicago at the ass crack of dawn to deal with a wage dispute at one of his distribution centers, but she'd been on his mind all day. He'd tried to work on the way to Chicago, but he kept checking his phone for an acknowledgment of the text he'd sent telling her he'd see her back at his office around six.

It was now six fifteen and fully dark as Hunt left his car and crossed the wet sidewalk to walk into the lobby of his building. Stepping into his private elevator, he tapped his foot irritably, wishing the damn thing would move faster.

If she wasn't sitting in his office waiting for him, he'd be seriously annoyed. So annoyed, in fact, that he might have to track her down at Kate's apartment. He needed to see her, dammit.

Need...

He didn't like that word. He'd trained himself as a child not to need or rely on anyone, not his mom or any of his foster parents. In his twenties, divorce and death reinforced the idea that he could only ever rely on himself. No, he *wanted* to see Adie. There was a huge difference between the two emotions.

Hunt rarely kept his staff working beyond five and when he stepped onto his floor, he saw that all the office lights were turned down low. The place was deserted, and he doubted Adie would stay in a strange, empty office.

Hunt stepped into his dark office and tossed his briefcase in the direction of his leather couch. Instead of the familiar *whoomp* he expected to hear, a low scream hit his ears, quickly followed by a curse. "Ow, ow, ow!"

Hunt's fist hit the light switch and he immediately looked toward the couch. Adie half lay on the couch, her long-sleeved black dress hiked to show off a very lovely leg. His briefcase rested in her lap and she rubbed her shoulder and glared at him.

"Why the hell did you do that?" Adie demanded, her eyes round and wide.

Hunt quickly crossed the room to reach her. He sat down on the edge of the couch, his thigh pressed into her hip. "Because I didn't expect you to be in my office, sitting on my sofa in the dark. Are you okay?"

Adie winced and prodded her shoulder with her fingertips. "I'm going to have a bruise."

"Do you need some ice?" Hunt asked, trying to think of a way he could move the tight round neck of her dress to inspect her shoulder.

"No, it's fine."

Damn.

Hunt lifted his briefcase off her lap, placed it on the floor and noticed Adie's heels were also on the floor, tipped on their side. His eyes flew over her—still gorgeous—but there was a head-sized indentation on the green throw pillow next to her. He looked at her, amused. "Were you asleep?"

Adie looked like he'd caught her rifling through his desk drawers. "I've been working long hours for weeks and weeks. Christmas is the busiest season for me. I was up at two this morning, dealing with a Japanese client who has bought a very rare, very expensive Samoyed puppy from a breeder in California."

"I've never heard of that breed," Hunt stated.

"I hadn't either and I asked my client about it, which was a huge mistake. He spent twenty minutes telling me about the puppy's bloodline and how much it cost."

"Give me the one-minute version."

"White, double-layer coat, originally from Siberia, intelligent, sociable and inquisitive. Very, very rare and this puppy cost the equivalent of a medium-sized car."

Hunt raised his eyebrows. "And you have to get it from California to Japan? How? In a crate?"

Adie's wide mouth curved and her smile hit her eyes. Hunt felt like he was witnessing the birth of a new star, the rearrangement of a faraway galaxy.

He sucked in a breath, looking for air.

"My clients' pets don't go in crates, Hunter. No, I found a dog walker who was prepared to collect the puppy and fly with him, on a private jet hired for the occasion, from Los Angeles to Osaka."

"Wow."

Adie pushed her hands through her hair and

tugged at the hem of her dress. "Anyway, I didn't get much sleep last night so I thought I'd just close my eyes for a minute. I didn't expect to get brained by a briefcase."

"I didn't expect you to be here," Hunt replied. Her hand went down to the hem of her dress and he captured the fabric between his thumb and index fingers, idly rubbing the soft material. "And, trust me, I have no problem looking at your legs."

Adie blushed, then sucked her bottom lip between her teeth. Her eyes, staring into his, were filled with a mixture of lust and confusion. He wondered which emotion would win.

"This is crazy, Hunt."

"Can't argue with that," Hunt agreed. "I take one look at you and all the blood in my brain heads south. All I can think about is getting you naked and making you mine."

Adie covered her face with her hands, but through the cracks in her fingers, he saw her complexion turn pink. He couldn't remember when last he'd seen a woman blush. It wasn't something that happened much anymore.

And Hunt was super curious to know how far down her blushes extended.

"I want you, Adie. You want me too."

"Well, duh," Adie muttered. "But it's not that simple, Hunt."

Hunt could see her looking for an excuse and knew she was going to say that he was her client, that they should be professional, that this could get complicated. Hunt decided to cut down her arguments before she could voice them. "We're old enough and smart enough to keep work and our attraction separate, Adie. One has nothing to do with the other."

"Theoretically," Adie replied. "But it never quite works out that way, does it?"

"If we want it to, it will," Hunt assured her. But instead of looking more relaxed, Adie's shoulders were up around her ears and she twisted a funky, vintage ring around the middle finger of her right hand. Something was really bugging her...

Oh, hell. Somehow Hunt knew she must've heard, or read, about Griselda's presence in his life and that she'd added two and two and reached pi.

Dammit.

Adie's next words confirmed his suspicions. "You have someone in your life, Hunt. And I don't like the idea of being the other woman."

Okay, he was going to strangle Kate with his bare hands because she was the only one who would've mentioned Griselda, the only person with the temerity to interfere in his business. The little brat!

"I don't have a relationship with Griselda."

Adie's eyebrows lifted, silently telling him not to BS her. "Not that there was anything to end, but I called it off a couple of days before I met you."

Adie cocked her head to the side. "How can you end something that is un-endable?"

Hunt smiled at her made-up word. And how could

he explain Griselda to Adie without sounding like a complete dog? Griselda had been convenient and Griselda considered him equally convenient... They were each a resource the other used. So much so that Griselda had propositioned him with the idea of being her sperm donor.

God, he'd barely given that idea, or Griselda, any thought since he'd met Adie. In fact, Adie was currently occupying all of his mental energy. It was a very unusual situation.

"It's over and done. Can we stop talking about her now?" Hunt demanded, sounding irascible.

Adie scooted down the couch behind him and found some space to swing her legs off. Her feet touched the floor and she stood up. Hunt stared at her as she slid her feet into a pair of bright orange heels.

Okay, when they made love she could keep those sexy shoes on...

"What do you want from me, Hunter?" Adie asked, walking over to his desk and sitting on the edge, her legs swinging.

Sex, maybe a couple of laughs, a fun way to end the year. Hunt believed in being upfront and honest, he didn't want to deal with hurt feelings or confusion. Sometimes, he was convinced that casual sex required more negotiation and emotional awareness than entering into a long-term relationship.

Hunt felt his nerves prickle and the moisture disappeared from his tongue. He felt ridiculous. He was a man in his thirties who had the right to just want some fun. Provided that Adie felt safe and was on board, they could have a great time.

Keep it simple and free of ambiguity.

"I was married once and it didn't work out." Okay, that wasn't where he'd planned to start his explanation and it wasn't relevant to the present situation. What the actual hell? He never discussed Joni, with anyone. He didn't like explaining to people that he'd been a fool.

"I'm sorry." Adie tipped her head to the side, obviously curious. "What happened?"

He wouldn't tell her. It was his business and not pertinent to this discussion. "She screwed around on me and was addicted to using my credit card."

God, now his mouth was operating without his brain's permission.

Adie winced. "She was a shopper."

That was like saying Usain Bolt was quite quick. Feeling like he had hands squeezing his neck, Hunt yanked his tie down and undid the button holding his collar closed. "I don't talk about her, about what happened."

Except that he had just expressed far more than he'd ever expressed before. To anyone. Hunt dismissed that thought and pushed his suit jacket back, his hands on his hips. "She's not pertinent to what we were talking about."

"That you have a girlfriend."

"I told you I ended it! I do not have a goddamn

girlfriend! Jesus!" Hunt gripped the bridge of his nose, hoping to squeeze his frustration away.

"Does Griselda live in Manhattan?"

Why was she asking? Did it matter? "She lives in the city but she's currently on the West Coast, she'll be there until Christmas. And none of this has anything to do with me wanting to sleep with you!"

Adie's huge round eyes met his. She put her thumbnail between her teeth and flicked it against her front tooth. Hunt wished she would end the torture and put him out of his misery. It wasn't difficult, he just required a yes or a no.

"I'm not sure, Hunt," Adie eventually told him.

Ah, well… *Hell.*

Adie gripped the desk on either side of her hips and Hunt fought the urge not to go to her. "I presume you are only offering a one night stand or a couple of one night stands, right?"

For some reason, his throat felt thick and tight and he couldn't force a yes up his throat. So Hunt nodded instead.

"Thought so." Adie hauled in a deep breath, then another. "Look, this is a pretty difficult time of year for me and sometimes, for complicated reasons I don't intend to explain, I've been known to look for a distraction, for something to help me through the season of love and goodwill to all men. That's the reason I am here, in Manhattan, during the busiest time of year for me…because I'm hoping to be so busy I can't think."

Hunt wanted to know what demons were nipping at her heels. What compelled her to keep herself so busy?

"But I don't use men to get me out of my head and between the work you've given me, my existing clients and trying to meet and sign up new clients, I am slammed."

Hunt watched her dark eyes and while she wasn't lying, she wasn't telling the complete truth either. Man, she fascinated him. On a deeper, darker and more dangerous level—a level he preferred to avoid.

Yet, he couldn't help thinking that she'd yet to say no.

"Are you saying no?" It was, after all, vital to be clear.

Adie nodded. "I'm saying no."

Hunt felt his stomach sink to his toes. Was that disappointment he felt? God, he'd been rejected before—not often, but it had happened—but it had never stung like this before. What was it about this slight, quirky woman who pulled unidentified and strange feelings to the surface?

One long kiss and she'd be begging for more...

So would he.

But he didn't want Adie like that. He wanted her to have no reservations, no second thoughts. He wanted her to be fully, utterly, wholly in the moment with him. Nothing less was acceptable. For that brief time, he wanted all of her and he wouldn't get it if she had the smallest doubt niggling at the edges of her mind.

Hell.

Adie jumped off the desk and walked over to the sofa. "It's been a long day and I have a bit of a headache. Do you mind if we get to work?"

Hunt was frustrated. He supposed he was spoiled. He'd never had to work this hard with Griselda, or any other woman. Once a man obtained a certain level of power, things usually came easy. Adie was anything but.

And, admittedly, she did look tired. Hunt could see the fatigue in her eyes, the strain around her mouth. He'd worked through fevers and migraines, and back when he'd been a professional ballplayer, he'd played with a cracked ankle and a concussion. Long story short, he never allowed anything to get in the way of what he needed to do. Maybe Adie was the same. But she obviously needed rest, an early night. If he suggested that she take off, he knew she'd insist on working.

Adie, he was coming to realize, had a helluva work ethic and a mile-wide stubborn streak.

"Look, I'm really beat and I've had a horrible day," Hunt lied. "Can we pick this up in the morning?"

As he knew it would, relief flashed through Adie's eyes. "Sure. I need to go over the final arrangements for the urban treasure hunt race with you tomorrow so I'll see you in the morning."

Hunt remembered that he had an early breakfast meeting and that the rest of his day was equally busy. "Sorry, I'm going to have to miss that. What about tomorrow evening, the same time again?"

Adie shook her head. "I promised Kate I'd go to her folks' house and be the referee as the Williams family argues about the best way to decorate Christmas cookies."

A long, hard shudder hit Hunt. Icing cookies plus memories of being with Steve and the Williams family was a combustible cocktail. "And you think that's a fun way to spend an evening?"

"I'm staying with Kate and it seemed rude not to accept the invitation," Adie replied. "Are you going?"

"I was invited, but no. You should know that Kate's clan is nosy and noisy and competitive and loud—"

Adie smiled. "Will there be wine?"

"Lots of wine. And Richard's eggnog, which is, I have to warn you, strong enough to strip the enamel off your teeth."

Adie clapped her hands, excited. "I love eggnog!"

It wouldn't take much for Adie, who didn't weigh more than a feather, to become intoxicated. Maybe he should go along to keep an eye on her...

"You're connected to Kate through her brother Steve, right?" Adie asked before Hunt could examine why he was feeling protective over this English girl who would be leaving the States in a couple of weeks.

Hunt nodded. "Yes, Steve and I played ball together. He was my best friend and business partner. He died a while back."

Hunt remembered attending the Williams clan's Christmas cookie bakeoff for years before Steve died. It had always been one of the happiest nights of his year. He'd enjoyed listening to the raucous, loving family argue and tease each other. They were the family he'd always dreamed of as a child. Many years had passed since Steve's death, but Hunter still received an invitation every year. He hadn't been back. He'd attended other functions with the Williams family, but he always found an excuse to miss the Christmas cookie bakeoff. And most of their other Christmas festivities too.

"I should make an effort to see them since it's been a while. But I prefer to meet them at restaurants or at neutral venues."

"Because being around them, in the place where you can visualize Steve, hurts too much?"

Exactly so.

Hunt expected her to dig for more, to put her fingers into the small crack he'd presented and widen the fissure, but Adie surprised him when her only reply was an understanding smile. Good. Because he had no intention of talking to her about Steve, about how gutted he still felt, how much he missed his friend, especially at this time of year.

Adie had dropped into his life, and in a few weeks, she'd drop out. One didn't talk about best friends and how much one missed them to people who wouldn't be permanent fixtures in one's life.

Okay, that meant not talking to anybody about Steve, but that was okay. Hunt wasn't a heart-to-heart-conversation kind of guy. What was the point of talking, anyway? Steve was gone and talking wouldn't bring him back, wouldn't replace what Hunt had lost.

A friend, a brother, a strong connection.

And the only conversation he was really interested in having with Adie consisted of whether or not she'd spend the night with him. Or a couple of nights. However, he phrased it, he just wanted a hell-yes, take-me-to-bed answer.

But he couldn't push, wouldn't.

"Can you look at your schedule and maybe carve out an hour for me sometime tomorrow afternoon?" Adie asked, breaking the silence between them. "I do need to get your input on a couple of issues."

Hunt did a mental review of his day and nodded. "Meet me here at five and I'll have you out of here by six, in plenty of time for the great cookie contest."

Adie nodded, dropped her head and stared at the floor. Then she looked past him to his view of Central Park and he saw the indecision on her face. What was she wrestling with? Whether to sleep with him or not? But her words, when they came, had no connection to what he wanted.

"I know this is none of my business but you should go, you know. To the cookie contest. No matter how hard it is. Kate talks about her twin a lot, Hunter, and how she and her family miss him," Adie continued, her smile sad. "As Kate told me, they not only lost Steve when he died, they also, sort of, lost you."

Hunt pushed back the lapels of his jacket to shove his hands into the pockets of his pants. His instinct was to snap at her, to tell her to mind her own business, that he was her client. That the only "getting personal" he wanted involved them shedding their clothes. And he could do that; he was enough of a bastard to get his point across. But, instead of pushing back, Hunter considered another response.

"He was the closest thing I had to a brother. And while he was alive, they were my family." He looked away, knowing his voice was close to cracking from the grief that was still, after so long, a living, breathing entity? Why was he telling her things he'd never been able to tell Kate or anyone else? Why was she able to pull his words to the surface?

"I think it's obvious they still consider you part of the family." Adie ran her hand down his arm, gripped his hand and squeezed. "Make cookies with them, Hunt. Even if you don't want to renew that close connection, it's a small thing that would give them a lot of pleasure. And it's the season to do good."

How could he resist those big brown expressive eyes? And, let's be honest here, if Adie was going to spend the evening with the Williams clan, then Hunt wanted to be there too. Something about her, more than lust and attraction, drew him.

Hunt, uncomfortable with the emotion swirling between them, mock shuddered. "Ugh, Christmas."

"Scrooge," Adie teased him. "I'm going to go." Pulling her hand from his, she walked toward the door and Hunt's eyes dropped from her luscious ass to her shapely legs. He could easily imagine his hands underneath her butt, those legs around his hips as he pushed into her.

He wanted her. Worse than that, he needed her.

Dammit. There was that word again.

"Adie?"

Her hand on the handle to the door, she turned. "Yeah?"

"Give my proposition some thought, okay? We'd be good together."

"Okay, I'll think about it."

Hunter squinted at her departing back, knowing that was as much as he was going to get from her.

For now.

She'd think about it?
Was she nuts?

Adie hailed a cab outside Hunt's building and gave the driver Kate's address. Then she asked herself why she hadn't flatly refused Hunt's straightforward offer. Oh, she knew why she wanted to say yes—he was volcano hot, she melted every time she got within thirty feet of him and she couldn't stop thinking about how good they'd be in bed—but no was the only possible answer.

Okay, she'd propositioned him the other night and, while it was completely out of character for her, it was still different from his offer fifteen minutes ago. On the night of the market they'd been two strangers. She'd hadn't known who he was. She'd thought it would be a "ships passing in the night" type of deal.

Uncharacteristic, sure but also uncomplicated. And instinctive…

She should've stuck to her guns, kept her no a no. Adie was mentally backtracking like mad. Sure, there were good and obvious reasons why she shouldn't sleep with him: he was her client, she wanted to do business with him in the future, she wanted him to recommend her to his rich friends and associates and she did not want to give the impression to him, or anyone, that she sealed the deal with sex.

And he'd recently ended his relationship with his long-term girlfriend. Adie wasn't interested in being the Band Aid to fix his dented ego.

Adie sighed and banged the back of her head against the seat of the taxi, reluctantly admitting that those were all valid excuses, even though they weren't the main reason why she should categorically refuse his offer.

Her hesitation was with Christmas. The feelings that bubbled up to the surface this time of year were so much stronger than at other times. From the middle of November until the New Year, these few weeks magnified and exacerbated all her fears and insecurities. The season was a trigger for her to indulge in excessive self-reflection about her past and to compare herself to other people who seemed to have more and do more.

She'd taught herself to drop her bad habits of looking for attention and validation in all the wrong places. For ten and a half months of the year she celebrated her single status, her commitment to her career, her ability to dash around the world and not have to explain to anyone where she was going or how long she'd be away. For roughly three hundred and thirty days a year, she reveled in her freewheeling lifestyle, completely content to be a wealthy, single woman with no pets, husband or children. For most of the year, she didn't give a thought to being partnerless or childless. She was content, happy even, to be on her own.

But at Christmastime...

God, the season slapped her silly. As soon as she saw the first decorated tree, the first string of Christmas lights, heard a favorite carol, the ghosts of Christmas past, present and future dropped by to say hi...

And soon they were whispering in her ear...

You should be looking for love. Wouldn't you like a child someday, someone to buy gifts for, to watch his face light with joy when he sees the presents Santa left on Christmas morning?

Look at this lovely advertisement of a family having fun together. And—look!—they even have a dog!

Don't you want a family like that? What about a dog? You'd like a dog...

Adie stared out the grimy window of the cab, oblivious to the Christmas decorations and the sleet touching the shoulders and heads of the pedestrians on the sidewalk. At this time of year, she tended to obsess about her parents and wonder why they couldn't love her, or show any interest in her, why her mom was so completely disinterested in being her mom. At Christmastime she had many "what if" thoughts—what if she had a husband, what if she had kids?

Would she feel happier, lighter, more fulfilled? Would having a family erase the hurt her parents caused? Did she really want to live the rest of her life being single? How long would flying all over the world, making her clients' lives easier, fulfill her?

Would she ever experience a love-filled, cozy Christmas?

She never felt like this in March or September, in August or at the beginning of spring. No, her descent into being maudlin and morose was directly linked to the festive season so right now, she had to stay objective, practical and unemotional.

Adie didn't want to backslide into bad habits so dating was out of the question. And having a festive fling when she wasn't as emotionally strong as she could be... It wasn't wise. She was a careful woman and she had no intention of walking through that minefield. She was vulnerable. This wasn't a good time of year for her and her usually impenetrable, keep-the-hell-out wall was a little cracked.

Sleeping with Hunt—with any man, but especially with Hunt—would be like handing him a sledge-hammer and pointing out the most brittle, easily broken bricks.

Nope, not happening. Not today, tomorrow or anytime soon. Not with Hunt or with anyone else.

Four

The next evening, Hunt found himself in Carnegie Hill, seated at the Williams' long dining table covered in a bright red tablecloth festooned with Santas, Christmas music playing in the background and a glass of whiskey was in easy reach.

In front of him was an oversized cookie in the shape of a Christmas tree; and multicolored bowls of frosting, sprinkles and sweets littered the length of the table.

Rachel Williams, bright-eyed and thoroughly excited, stood at the head of the table, the wine in her glass sloshing with every gesture she made. Kate looked more like her mom than ever before, Hunt noticed.

"Quiet! Quiet!"

Hunt looked around the table and smiled as ten faces turned in her direction. Mike, the youngest was flying single at tonight's Christmas event—he was, per Kate, an even bigger player than Steve had been and that was saying something. But Grant, the oldest brother, was married and had a two-year-old girl, Bella, and a four-year-old boy, Cayden. Cayden was sitting on Kate's lap and nobody but Hunt seemed to notice the kid was sneaking pieces of his already-broken Christmas tree cookie to Rachel's Maltese poodle sitting under the table.

Hunt's eyes moved to Adie. Like him, she was still dressed in her work clothes, a white button-down shirt and black pants, severe but oh-so sexy. He ran a hand over his face. Sitting across from her, being here, felt right, like this moment was long overdue.

That being said, it was still overwhelming. He wasn't used to so much noise: people talking over each other and the Christmas carols in the background. To Hunt, it felt like someone had dialed up the volume on his life, and he couldn't help looking around for Steve, convinced his friend was in the kitchen or just around the corner. Then Hunt remembered Steve was dead and it was a gut punch.

Hunt had made a habit of distancing himself from this much emotion. He'd made a habit of forcing it down, pushing it away, and at work he could easily do that. He and Steve might've started the company shortly after they both retired from professional sports, but Hunt had managed and grown the business over the past ten years without his friend. The memories of Steve at work weren't strong.

In this house, they were everywhere.

His being here tonight had to be hard for the family too, but they weren't acting like it. When Rachel opened her front door and saw him standing there with Adie, tears leaked from her eyes. She'd pulled him into a hug, not letting go for the longest time. Richard, a little more stoic, shook Hunt's hand and clapped his shoulder, and Grant and Mike greeted him like they'd seen him yesterday. Hunt felt guilty for avoiding this particular tradition, all their Christmas functions, and felt equally guilty for not spending more time with them than he had.

He'd missed them and they'd, apparently, missed him back. It felt good. Weird. But good.

Rachel banged her spoon on the table to make her noisy family stop talking and Richard reached up and gently removed the glass of wine from her hand. He placed it on the table and looked at Hunt, who was sitting to his right.

"She's the clumsiest creature alive and this carpet frequently looks like a crime scene."

Rachel tapped his shoulder with her spoon. "Hush now."

Richard rolled his eyes at Hunt and turned his attention back to his wife. Rachel made eye contact with everyone at the table individually before speaking. "I've changed the Family Cookie Contest rules—"

"Are you allowed to do that without our consent?" Kate cheekily asked her.

"Yeah, Mom, can you do that? Isn't this family run as a democracy?" Grant asked, purely, Hunt decided, to wind Rachel up. Grant was braver than he could ever be. Rachel was tiny but she was fierce.

"This family is not, in any shape or form, a democracy. Since I spent twelve or more hours in labor with every one of you, I am your supreme ruler," Rachel retorted, but Hunt heard the affection in her voice.

"That's pretty accurate actually," Richard commented, his tone dry as dust.

Rachel narrowed her eyes at him. "In front of you is a giant tree cookie and participation is mandatory…everyone has to decorate one."

"And how do we judge the winner?" Kate demanded. Hunt heard the competitive streak in her voice and smiled. God, she and Steve were so alike.

"We take photos of our trees and we share them on social media. The tree with the most likes is the winner."

"That's not fair, Hunt has a pretty big fan base," Kate whined. "He's famous."

After much discussion about the rules and deadlines and how to count the likes—and after giving him a handicap—Rachel finally gave her family permission to start decorating their cookies. Hunt, not having a creative bone in his body looked at the bowls of frosting and the piping bag at his elbow and shook his head. With Duncan out of the office, Hunt was incredibly busy and yet he was sitting here about to pipe icing on cookies.

But, honestly, there was no place he'd rather be.

Adie flashed him a smirky smile and expertly twisted her piping bag so that the white frosting filled one corner of the bag. "Watch and learn."

Hunt followed her directions and soon had his cookie covered in white frosting. He reached for a bowl of chocolate buttons and placed them around the edge of the tree, pleased by his efforts.

He popped a button into his mouth, caught Adie's eye and instantly remembered the exceptional one-of-a-kind chocolates he'd tasted a few days back. "Well, it's not chili and bacon," he told her when she met his gaze.

Adie blushed, but before she could respond, Grant directed a question at him. "Kate's been telling me about your foundation's urban treasure hunt. It was an inspired idea to team celebrities with teenagers from the foundation's sports programs. And running through the city sounds amazing. You're going to have such a good time."

Hunt shook his head. "Oh, I'm not running."

Everyone turned to look at him and he frowned at their perplexed faces. He lifted his hands in the air. "What? Why are you all looking at me like that?"

"I thought you were part of a team. Why on earth aren't you participating?" Adie voiced the question they all, obviously, wanted the answer to.

Actually, that was a damn good question. Why wasn't he running in his own damn race? Running was something he enjoyed but, like so much, it was way down his list of priorities. Work, and more work, filled positions one to five.

Work was all he did.

Hunt wriggled, uncomfortable with the way the Williams clan, including the kids, were looking at him. Adie just sat in her chair, smiling at his discomfort.

He didn't have a decent excuse and he didn't want to tell them that the thought of running hadn't occurred to him. "I'm too busy, even more so than normal because Duncan is out of the office and my workload is intense."

"It's a couple of hours on Saturday, Hunter, and everybody, including you, deserves some downtime," Adie told him, resting her forearms on the table, her elbow precariously close to her glass of eggnog. He reached across the table and moved the glass to a safer spot.

"Even if it was something I wanted to do—" and to be honest, he kinda, sorta, did want to "—I can't enter because I don't have someone to run it with me. The kids involved have already been matched with the athletes and have, hopefully, started to develop a relationship with their mentors."

"It's your race, you can add someone to the registration roll or you can run with whomever you want to," Kate said.

True. He mentally thought through some of his acquaintances and ex-teammates and realized they were either already partaking in the race or had previous commitments. "Steve would be my go-to person," Hunt quietly stated. There, he'd mentioned Steve's name. For the first time in a decade, he'd brought Steve into the conversation. Hunt felt Richard's hand on his shoulder, the manly squeeze. Talking about Steve was hard, but damn, he deserved to be part of the conversation.

Hunt looked at Rachel and, on seeing the tears in her eyes, quickly looked away. God, if she started crying, he wouldn't be able to bear it.

"Since the foundation is named after Steve, what about one of Steve's brothers running with Hunt?" Adie's brisk question cut through the tension.

Grant shook his head. "I'd love to but we're leaving to go out of town tomorrow."

Adie looked at Mike, who shook his head. "Sorry, I'm unavailable too."

Kate pouted. "I see nobody asked me."

Adie patted her back. "Honey, your idea of exercise is binge-watching a series on Netflix."

"Funny," Kate retorted.

When their laughter died down, Hunt shrugged, ignoring his spurt of disappointment. "It's not a big deal and I really should work. I'll be at the start and then I'll see everyone at the cocktail party later."

"I'll be your partner."

Hunt's eyes flew back to Adie, as did everyone else's. "What? Why?"

"It sounds like fun," Adie told him. "I get to run around Manhattan chasing down clues in odd places. It'll be awesome!"

"It's a seven-mile race," Hunt pointed out.

"I used to run cross-country as a kid and, at university I loved running marathons. I still, occasionally manage a five-mile run on the treadmill. Pfft, I'll be fine," Adie said, brushing off his concerns over her fitness.

"But won't you be busy organizing the day?" Hunt asked her.

Kate answered for Adie. "Nope, the events company is in charge from the moment the teams arrive at the morning start. And Adie's already delegated the awards dinner and dance following the race to me so I'll be around and able to deal with any last-minute problems."

Hunt looked at Adie and saw the challenge in her eyes. Laughter tipped up the edges of her mouth. "What, Sheridan, are you scared that one of your old teammates, or one of the younger kids, might beat you, a New York native?" she teased.

No, he wasn't scared because that was never going to happen. He pointed his piping bag at Adie. "You'd better not slow me down."

"Pfft, you'd better not slow *me* down. And my tree cookie is way better than yours."

Hunt looked down at his tree and saw that the

white frosting had slid off, taking six chocolate buttons with it. He scowled at Adie, who just grinned. Unable to resist her impish face, he flicked a button across the table in her direction.

"Hunter Sheridan, we do not throw food!" Rachel scolded him and Hunt felt like he was nineteen again. It was both terrifying and reassuring.

"Yes, ma'am."

As the conversation moved on, Hunt looked around the table at the large, loving family and contrasted their affection, their obvious enjoyment in being with each other with what Griselda had proposed—loveless co-parenting with their child being raised more by a nanny than by them. If he ever had a child, he wanted to raise it within a tight, loving, noisy, affectionate family and that would require him to make a commitment, to relinquish his freedom, to give up control.

He couldn't do it, not now, not ever. He'd worked so hard to create a world where he felt comfortable operating. He preferred keeping women, all people, at a distance.

Hunter briefly wondered how Griselda's West Coast trip was going and shrugged away his curiosity. Their road together had split into two forks, one for him and one for her. He was okay with that. Everything had its season after all.

Hunt looked across the table at Adie, who was deep in conversation with Rachel. If he had to equate women to seasons then Griselda was winter, but Adie was spring. Bright, vibrant, interesting...*new*.

But still just a season, and his time with her, when he finally got her into bed, would pass quickly.

She'd move on and so would he because nothing lasted forever.

When Adie suggested she be Hunt's partner for the Amazing Race–style treasure hunt across Manhattan, she'd thought it would be a small event, with them mostly running through Central Park.

Choosing to concentrate on buying Hunt's gifts for his business colleagues, staff and friends and organizing his corporate Christmas events, and keeping up with the never ending requests from her existing clients, Adie had handed most of the race related work over to Kate and had minimal input into the foundation's event. As a result, she hadn't taken in many of the details.

The race, she'd quickly realized when she arrived at the starting point, was bigger and bolder than anything she expected. There were reporters and news crews, and crowds of onlookers were contained behind the tape. And while they were starting the race in the park, they'd be winding their way through Midtown before heading for lower Manhattan.

So far today she'd seen an Olympic figure skater, a world-class swimmer, lots of famous basketball players, golfers and many baseball players. Their teenage running mates looked wide-eyed and excited.

While she'd been a runner in school and was naturally fit, she'd forgotten that Hunt had once been a world-class athlete. She'd also forgotten to take into consideration that Hunt's legs were a lot longer than hers. And, as he'd told her at the starting line, he regularly ran ten miles.

And competitive, dear Lord, he was competitive!

They were in Chelsea on the fourth of seven legs and Adie, breathing heavily, was dodging tourists and residents, trying and failing, to keep up with Hunt's long-legged stride. They were, as far as they knew, in either second or third place and Hunt was determined to be first. He was the head of the foundation, he'd reminded her, he needed to lead by example.

His leading by example might just kill her, but whatever.

It wasn't in his nature to trail behind anyone, Adie thought, keeping her eye on his broad back in the insulated lime green running tops they both wore. He hadn't created a massive business empire by allowing other people to take the lead. No, he was determined and driven and he fought for what he wanted. And today he wanted to win, and if he had to drag Adie to the finish line, half-dead, then that was what he'd do.

Adie was starting to think that death was a distinct possibility.

Hunt stopped and waited for her to catch up, his hands on his hips. Damn but his running tights should be declared illegal, she decided. The material clung to his muscled thighs and running behind him, catching glimpses of his perfect ass, was one of the few high points of this freezing day.

She wanted coffee, she wanted her parka, she wanted to lie down and sleep for a week. Really, she was too old to run at such a fast pace without much training.

She wasn't sixteen anymore.

"Can you see the sports memorabilia store?" Hunt demanded when she reached him.

So that was what they were looking for. She'd forgotten. Looking around the quaint shops, her attention was caught by a vintage jewelry shop across the road, its window filled with the unusual and the quirky. Knowing it was her type of shop, Adie instinctively stepped off the sidewalk to cross the road but Hunt grabbed her top and hauled her back to his side.

"That's not a sports memorabilia store."

Well, no, but this store was more her style. She needed five minutes, just to see whether it was worth another visit. Hunt scowled at her suggestion. "We're running a race, Ashby-Tate!"

"Five minutes can't hurt," Adie said, using her most cajoling tone.

"I know those eyes of yours could convince a monk to give up his vows of celibacy but they won't work on me, not today," Hunt told her, looking past her to scan the street. He lifted his arm and pointed. Adie saw a half-concealed sign showing just the first four letters of *Sport*.

Adie felt Hunt tug her down the street and she sent a look over her shoulder, mentally committing the name of the shop to memory because Mr. Competitive couldn't give her five minutes.

Hunt allowed her to walk for about ten yards and when they could see all of the sign saying they'd found the right store, he broke into a fast jog. Adie, trailing behind him, leaped over a small dog on a leash in her haste to meet Hunt, who'd found the event company staffer. He stood next to a huge vertical banner advertising Hunt's foundation and wore a red-and-green elf hat and pointy ears. A few feet from him a Santa Claus held a transparent bowl and collected donations from the Christmas shoppers and pedestrians. A small crowd had gathered in the hope of seeing some of their favorite sports stars.

Hunt greeted the young man and held out his hand for the next clue. The staffer, wearing a lime green Williams-Sheridan Foundation sweatshirt similar to their running tops, gave them a genial smile. "Hey, there, are you having a good run? Let's take the photograph and get you on your way."

Hunt removed his phone from the pouch on his bicep and prepared to take a photograph of the three of them, proof that they'd made the stop and at what time.

"Uh, where's your bobblehead?"

Hunt frowned at the young man's question and looked at Adie. Adie lifted her hands in an I-don't-have-a-clue gesture. "What are you talking about?"

"Each team was given a bobblehead figure at the start of the race and you are supposed to have the figure in every photograph. If you don't, you'll get disqualified."

Adie recalled the bobblehead figure someone handed to her and remembered Hunt saying it was Babe Ruth and he'd bring them luck. She'd left Babe, as far as she knew, on the table next to the young woman at the second stop, which was way back on the Lower East Side.

Hunt released a series of curses and placed his hands behind his head, gray eyes frustrated. "You are goddamn kidding me."

"Sorry, I'm not. If you don't have the bobblehead, you'll be disqualified."

"Why the hell didn't the other guys giving clues tell us that?" Hunt demanded.

The kid shrugged. "They might be new or maybe they just forgot."

They'd been doing so well so far and, because she'd left the bobblehead, all their efforts were in vain. Adie placed her hand on Hunt's chest and stared up into his light eyes. "I'm so sorry, Hunt, I messed up."

Instead of yelling at her as she expected him to do, he just lowered his arms and dredged up a smile. "It's just a race, right?" He looked at the kid. "Can we carry on without the bobblehead?"

"Yeah, but you're technically disqualified. But you know, you are the main dude so you'd probably still be in the running." The kid smiled. "I mean, it's not like they're going to boot you out, right?"

Adie instantly knew that didn't sit well with Hunt. He wanted to win, but he wanted to do it on a fair playing field. He didn't want any special favors. She respected the hell out of him just for that. As much as she wanted to hail a taxi, get out of this freezing wind and stop somewhere for a hot cup of chocolate, she knew they had to finish the race, as a point of pride. He was representing a foundation that was founded on hard work, fairness and equity and he had to lead by example.

"Let's carry on. We'll tell them we're disqualified, but at least we will have finished." Adie suggested.

Hunt looked down at her and shook his head. "I'm going back."

Adie's mouth dropped open. "What do you mean?"

"I'm going to run back, get the bobblehead and then we'll finish the race." He shrugged. "I need to show the kids that you can't cut corners, that a job worth doing is worth doing properly." He looked at the young man, who'd pulled his elf hat over his pink ears. "Can I leave my partner here? It'll be faster if I do it on my own."

He shook his head, regretful. "Either you both do it and get the photos, or you'll be disqualified."

Hunt winced, obviously disappointed. He cursed again, his shoulders slumping. After a minute he looked at Adie. "Okay then, we'll do it your way. Ready to run disqualified?"

Adie, knowing she'd regret this later, shook her head. "Nope."

It was impossible to miss the disappointment in Hunt's eyes. "You want to give up?"

Adie shook her head. "Nope, we're going back, both of us, together. I'm going to bitch and whine but if it means finishing the race properly, then that's what we do."

The tender expression in Hunt's eyes nearly dropped her to her knees. "You've already run four miles, Adie, and the temperature is dropping. We don't have to do this. By the time we're done, we would've run nearly ten miles."

Dear God, no. They could run disqualified, Adie thought. It was a stupid mistake, people made mistakes, even brilliant, driven CEOs. Or their personal concierges. People would understand.

But instead of begging him to carry on, a different sentence came out of her mouth.

"Would you be going back if you were on your own?" Adie asked him, her tone challenging.

Hunt slowly nodded. "Yeah, I would."

Dammit, she'd known that was exactly what he'd say. Adie stamped her feet and blew on her hands. "Well then, the quicker we turn around, the quicker we'll get to the finish line. Last, I'm sure, but we'll do it properly." She smiled at Hunt. "There had better be hot chocolate at the end, Sheridan or I won't be happy."

Hunt dropped a quick openmouthed kiss on her lips. "I'm sure there will be. But if you want something special, I'll call ahead and arrange that. Wasabi or bacon and chili?"

"Plain is fine, but there had better be a vat of it."

Hunt gave her a quick hug and Adie soaked up his warmth. Taking his hand, they broke into a slow jog and headed back in the direction they came.

Oh, she was so going to regret this in the morning. Or in fifteen minutes.

Five

Hunt, standing within a group including the Monarchs' manager and captain, looked across the art deco music hall. With the arrival of the celebrities and sports stars and their significant others, the hall was filled to capacity. A DJ shared the stage with a huge Christmas tree and the dance floor was crowded.

The buffet-style food had been demolished and the bartenders were hopping. It had been a long day, one that would be talked about for a long time to come and Hunt had had as much fun as everyone else. Okay, he and Adie, thanks to their stupid mistake, had taken forever to complete the route, but they'd been only ten minutes behind the last competitor. Frankly, considering they'd run another half race, they'd kicked ass.

Of course, that hadn't stopped the teasing from his ex-teammates and sports colleagues. They'd been, as he expected, ruthless. But under the teasing, he'd heard respect and that meant more to Hunt than anything else.

And he wouldn't have been able to do it without Adie.

Adie had immediately picked up on his need to do the race right, and she'd been at his side, or a few steps behind him, the whole way. Despite her threat to bitch and whine, she'd done neither, just put her head down and got the job done.

His respect for her was through the roof.

Griselda would never have considered running; it would've been beneath her. In fact, when he'd first proposed the urban treasure hunt race as a way to raise funds for his foundation, she'd told him he was better served overseeing the event and micromanaging the event coordinators to make sure nothing went wrong. Griselda, he'd recently realized, fed his appetite for control while Adie, well, with Adie he simply had fun.

God, he couldn't remember when last he'd felt so light around a woman. Or smiled so much. She was easy to be with; Adie didn't make small talk but when she spoke, he was immediately interested in everything she had to say. She was, in every way he could think of, the exact opposite of Griselda.

Griselda…

Hunt pushed his hand inside his jacket to pull out his phone and abruptly stopped, telling himself he didn't need to read the message again. He knew the words by heart.

While I didn't think your follow-up call confirming the end of our relationship was necessary, thank you for the courtesy. I hope, someday, we can resume our friendship.

So stiff and so formal, just like their relationship. Hunt briefly closed his eyes and knew the strange feeling pumping through him was a sense of relief. Griselda was, officially and definitely, part of his past. And, while he'd always considered himself single, nothing bound him and Griselda together. He felt lighter, brighter, happier, like a snake who'd shed too tight a skin.

Maybe it was time to make more changes, to re-evaluate his life, to start looking outside of work for ways to fill his hours. He'd loved today, being outside, exercising but also interacting with the volunteers, teenagers and sports celebrities. He should start doing more races, maybe a triathlon or two. Or maybe the foundation could organize urban treasure hunts in other cities.

He should brainstorm his idea with Adie and Kate, see whether they could translate his vague idea into an actionable plan. His excitement dropped several levels when he realized that Adie would be leaving soon, that she wasn't going to be in the city for more than a couple of weeks. Dammit.

Ignoring the cold fingers squeezing his lungs, he looked around the room. Speaking of his sexy teammate, where was she?

Hunt searched for her and eventually found her standing in the corner opposite him. She wasn't hard to spot, in a room of women mostly wearing neutral shades, her wide-legged green pants and matching wraparound top were the exact color of a Christmas tree. The brilliant green highlighted her creamy, flawless complexion and dark, ruffled hair. He normally liked long hair on a woman, but Adie's short hair suited her pixie face.

God, she was gorgeous.

And he wasn't the only one who noticed…

Thirty minutes ago, she'd been deep in conversation with Maxwell Green, a newly retired basketball legend. Before that he'd caught her laughing at whatever Blake, soccer's hottest player this season, had been telling her. Now she was leaning against the far wall, and his brand ambassador's hand— the man whose salary he paid to promote Sheridan Sports—was flat on the wall above her head as he loomed over her…

But Adie wasn't objecting. If anything, she was enjoying Liam Pearson's attention far too much. Yeah, not happening.

Hunt didn't bother excusing himself from the group, he just pushed his way through the crowd and within minutes stood behind Pearson, his arms crossed. Adie was the first to notice him and, instead of moving away from Pearson, she just raised her eyebrows. "Something I can help you with, Hunter?"

Hunter rocked on his heels and gritted his teeth as Pearson took his time lifting his hand off the wall and creating distance between him and Adie.

"Boss," Pearson murmured.

Hunt saw irritation flicker through the man's eyes at being interrupted and he narrowed his eyes at Pearson. In ten seconds, hopefully less, Pearson would realize that Adie wasn't another of his many conquests, that she wasn't someone who'd be another notch on his extremely scarred bedpost.

Hunt held his eyes.

Ten seconds passed, then fifteen and Hunt saw Adie eyes jumping between his face and Pearson's and after twenty seconds—Pearson liked to push boundaries—the man lifted his hands in defeat. Turning to Adie, he sent her a regretful smile. "It's been lovely talking to you, Adie."

Adie tossed a puzzled look at his back and when her eyes met Hunt's, she scowled. "What just happened?"

If she didn't know, then he wasn't going to elucidate.

"Hunter?"

Oh, okay, then. Hunt jammed his hands into the pockets of his soft black pants. "He was chatting you up and was about to ask you out on a date."

"That much I understood," Adie retorted.

There! That! Her going out on a date was not going to happen.

When he told her so, fury—hot and wild—sparked in her eyes. "And why would you think, for one bloody minute, that's your decision to make?" Adie demanded, her voice cold.

Because dates lead to intimacy and the only person he could imagine getting naked with Adie was *him*. Yeah, call him a Neanderthal or overbearing or ruthless, but he was the only man who'd kiss that wide mouth, explore the dip of her waist, slide his fingers between her feminine folds.

Adie slapped her arms across her chest and tapped her foot in annoyance. "Waiting for an explanation of your high-handedness, Sheridan. I might be working for you, but your authority over me does not extend to who I date!"

Hunt realized their argument was garnering attention. Looking around, he noticed a dark passageway to the right of them, clearly marked Staff Only. Judging by the lack of light, it wasn't being used, but it would be a perfect place to get his point across.

Conscious of his strength, he gently gripped Adie's narrow wrist and tugged her down the passageway, stopping when the hallway turned and they were out of sight of the party. Hunt placed his hand under Adie's elbows and easily lifted her off her feet, turning so his back shielded her from anyone who might amble down the hallway. Lowering her to her feet, he watched as she pushed her back into the wall, her eyes dark and mysterious in the low light spilling in from the music hall.

Adie, because she was as feisty as hell, lifted her chin. "Still waiting for an apology, Sheridan. Or an explanation as to why we are here."

Hunt slapped his hands on the wall on either side of her head, his eyes bouncing from her eyes to her red mouth. "You're not going to get an apology. And you know damn well why we are here."

In the small space he'd left between them, Adie gestured to the hallway. "I'm in the dark, literally and metaphorically."

He'd seen the flash of awareness in her eyes, noticed that her gaze kept dropping to his mouth.

"Stop being coy, Adie. You know I want to kiss you, I've been wanting to kiss you all damn day. And I'm sure you want to kiss me back."

He expected a sarcastic retort, a denial, for her to play hard to get, but Adie's hand moved up his arm, onto his shoulder to curl around the back of his neck. She further surprised him by reaching up onto her tiptoes and placing her lips against his, sighing as their mouths connected.

Hunt dropped his head and pushed his hand between the wall and her slim back, pulling her into him so that her breasts pushed into his chest, her stomach into his hard-as-hell erection.

He wanted her with a desperation that bordered on irrationality.

Unable to delay gratification for a millisecond longer, Hunt lifted his thumb to the adorable dip in the middle of her bottom lip and pressed down gently. "Open up, sweetheart, I need to taste you."

Adie's gentle breath drifted over his thumb, hit his lips and Hunt covered her mouth with his, seeking her tongue. She tasted of chocolate and white wine, smelled of hyacinths and heaven. Hunt's senses went into overdrive: his nose filled with her delicious scent, her mouth was a gourmet's paradise, he heard every sigh she uttered. Her body, under his roving hands, was feminine and slim, with subtle curves begging him to explore more.

In that moment, Adie was everything he needed or could ever want.

Hunt's hand curved around her bottom and she tilted her hips up to rub against the rod in his pants and Hunt felt a little lightheaded, probably because every drop of blood was heading south. After skimming his hand over her butt and down again, he bent his legs and easily lifted her off her feet.

Pushing her into the wall, Hunt groaned when his cock rested against her mound and watched as she tipped her head back to rest against the wall, exposing her elegant neck. "You are so very beautiful," Hunt told her, dropping his lips onto the cord on the right side of her neck. He nibbled gently, not wanting to leave a mark on her, and allowed his lips to move up to that sensitive spot where her jaw met her ear before tugging her earlobe into his mouth.

"Damn, I'd really like to take you to bed."

Adie tensed in his arms and Hunt winced, knowing his words had broken the spell. He never spoke without thinking but Adie had him tied up in knots.

Adie slid down the wall and when she stood on her feet again, Hunt took a small step back, but kept his hand on her waist. He couldn't not touch her—after a soul-melting kiss, that was asking the impossible.

Adie pushed a trembling hand through her hair before placing her fingertips on her lips, closing her eyes.

"Dear God, Sheridan, you know how to kiss."

Did he? Or had he just upped his game because he was kissing her? "Right back at you, sweetheart."

Adie took a tiny step and placed her forehead on his chest, the top of her head fitting under his chin. She gripped handfuls of his shirt in both hands and Hunt waited for their breathing to even out. It could take minutes or days, he didn't care, he was just happy to be standing here with her in his arms.

Of course, he'd be far happier if they were in a bed naked…

"We should get back, people will be wondering where you are."

"Don't wanna," Hunt replied, dropping a kiss in her hair. He wouldn't push her, this still had to be her decision.

He sensed Adie's lips curling into a smile. "Now, be a big boy, Hunter."

Hunt gripped her hips and pulled her into him,

pushing her stomach against his still-impressive erection. "I am a big boy."

Adie's laugh was low and sexy and sparks ignited over every inch of his skin. Then, dammit, she placed her hands on his chest and created a foot of distance between them. But her hands, Hunt noticed, remained on his chest. She seemed to be having as hard a time letting him go as he was releasing her.

Good to know. They could be home in thirty minutes, naked in thirty-one… "Come home with me, Adie."

Adie stared down at the toe of her black shoe peeking out from under her wide-legged pants. "It's not a good idea, Hunter."

Hunt felt irrationally angry and deeply disappointed. They weren't feelings he was accustomed to. As a ballplayer, he'd never been short of offers and when he'd had his fill of stranger sex—it got old quicker than he thought it would—he hooked up with friends who knew the score: a good time, no commitment and no drama. Then he met Griselda. Over the last few months, their sexual encounters had been sporadic at best. And uninspiring. It was no more her fault than his, but the truth was that, at the end, the spark between them was already dying.

Unlike the roaring wildfire burning between him and Adie.

"Please don't give me that tired excuse of us working together. Give me a decent reason because I know you want me and I sure as hell want you." Hunt rubbed her cheekbone with the pad of his thumb. "What can I say to change your mind?"

Adie fiddled with the bow at her waist and Hunt, knowing that a small tug would be the starting point to undressing her, wished she wouldn't. "Honestly, I'm sure there are a dozen things you could say that would change my mind—"

Now, this was interesting. "Like what?"

Adie wrinkled her nose and ignored his hopeful question. "Can I be honest with you?"

Sure, honesty was one of his favorite things. "Go ahead."

"Christmas is a bad time of year for me," Adie said, her voice low. "For most of the year, I'm a badass..."

He had to smile at that, he couldn't imagine Adie taking names and kicking ass.

Adie placed her hand on his waist and he flinched when she lightly pinched him. "Don't you laugh at me! I really am! I'm strong and confident and happy. I enjoy going out and having a good time."

Hunt tensed, not liking the idea of Adie having a good time without him. And what exactly was that good time comprised of? Sleeping with guys? Yeah, the thought did not thrill him.

Hunt ran his fingers through his hair, irritated with himself. He wasn't a hypocrite, if men could enjoy themselves in the bedroom so could women, without any guilt or stigma. He knew that, intellectually, but the thought of Adie having random affairs made his teeth slam together.

Yet, a quick affair was all he could offer her. Ironic, right?

"I'm committed to being single, to not being answerable to anyone, to not being married, having a partner or having kids."

Despite her tough words, Hunt thought he heard wistfulness in her voice. "You sound like you're trying to convince yourself not me."

"Ah!" Adie drilled her finger into his chest and Hunt captured it. "In July or February, we would probably be in bed together but it's Christmas…"

Okay, he'd lost her. "What does Christmas have to do with us sleeping together?"

"It's *Christmas*, Hunter!"

"I need a bit more of an explanation than you telling me over and over that's it's Christmas, Adie."

Adie's shoulders reached her ears. "When I was a lot younger, I had a history of using men to satisfy my need for attention and validation. I'd jump into relationships fast and, inevitably, would end up with a broken heart."

Hunt didn't know where she was going with this but he'd listen. Listen, and try to understand—that was all he could do.

"I cured myself of doing that and I've been celibate for a long, long time."

"How long?" Hunt asked.

"Five years."

"Hot damn," Hunt replied. "But I'm still not seeing the connection between you saying no to me, your past and Christmas."

"I'm not sure if I'm attracted to you because, you know, chemistry." Adie pushed her hand through her hair, looking miserable. "Or if I'm looking for attention or if I'm using you as a distraction to push away a lot of bad memories. They always seem to float to the surface at this time of year."

"Can you share those memories with me?" Hunt asked, curious.

"I'm sorry, I can't. I'm scared that, by sleeping with you, I'd be jumping back into an old habit and that I might start confusing attraction for attention again."

Hunt immediately understood the subtext to her words. "You're worried you are going to confuse sex and affection?" He wouldn't say the word love—it had no place in this conversation.

Or in his life.

Adie stared at the floor, her arms crossed over her chest, her mouth thin with embarrassment.

Hunt lifted her chin and waited for her to meet his eyes. "I'm not the guy you want to fall in love with, Adie. I don't do love, commitment, happy-ever-after. I don't believe in the concept."

Adie threw up her hands, frustrated. "Yeah, I understand that. I don't either, Hunter! That's why I'm trying to figure out what I'm feeling, why I need to keep saying no to sleeping with you."

"Look, I know myself really well and, frankly,

this has little do with you and everything to do with me," Adie added.

He heard her "get over yourself" subtext as clearly as if she'd spoken the words. Oh, and that was something else he found so damn attractive about her—he didn't intimidate her. Neither did he put stars in her eyes.

"You're an attractive, successful, interesting guy but I'm also leaving soon and we are working together and it's all too complicated."

Adie rested her forehead on his collarbone. "Trust me, Sheridan, I'm wickedly tempted but I learned, a long time ago, that nobody is going to look after me. It's up to me to protect myself. This is me, protecting myself."

I'd like to protect you.

Hunt lifted his hand to rub his lower jaw, feeling a little unbalanced from that very unusual and left-of-center thought. But for the first time in his adult life, he wanted to stand between a woman and whatever caused her pain. He wanted to protect Adie from whatever threatened her, whether it was self-doubt or her past or some existential threat.

He wanted to wrap her in his arms and hold her tight, putting his back to the world and taking the hits for her.

Holy crap.

Hunt didn't recognize himself. This wasn't who he was, this wasn't who he wanted to be. Adie had him tied up in knots; around her, he was the human equivalent of an intricately tangled ball of Christmas lights.

The real Hunt, the Hunt he was comfortable with—free, decisive, commitment-phobic—never spent this much time talking to or thinking about a woman.

But Adie, whether she was with him or not, was always front and center and…

He didn't like it.

Not one bit.

But, dammit to hell and back, he really liked her.

Adie patted his chest before stepping back. "Let's just take a deep breath here, Sheridan. Hell, in a day or two you might find me bloody annoying and you'll be desperate to get rid of me."

"I doubt that," Hunt murmured, not being able to visualize feeling that way.

"Or I might find that you are actually a huge jerk under that gorgeous body and hot face."

Now that was much more likely.

On Sunday morning, and after a night reliving Hunt's truly excellent kiss, Adie stood under the portico of The Stellan, which was one of the most iconic apartment buildings in Manhattan. Like the Eldorado, it was constructed in the thirties and was an art deco masterpiece.

Adie found it hard to believe that Hunt owned not one, but all the apartments in this building. Most he used as office space, the penthouse was his living space and the floor separating his work and personal space was an apartment used for visitors. His view of Central Park, while not as wild as the vistas from Ashby Hall overlooking the sandy beaches of western Wales, had to be amazing.

Adie rocked on the heels of her over-the-knees brown suede boots and wished Hunt had invited her up to his apartment instead of offering to meet her outside. She would love to see where he lived, but knew that if she stepped into his apartment, she had a very good chance of becoming intimately acquainted with his bedroom.

Which wouldn't be the worst place to be on a Sunday morning…

Had she been in her early twenties, that was exactly where she'd be this morning. Lying there naked with stars in her eyes, mentally redecorating his bedroom, wondering what to cook him for dinner or whether they'd have a boy or a girl first.

Yeah, she'd gotten that carried away before. To be honest, she'd been, on the odd occasion, worse than that. She'd once, okay, maybe a few times, flat out begged her boyfriend not to leave her.

It had not been pretty.

Looking back on the desperate, sad, intense girl she'd been was difficult. It made her cringe, but it was necessary because she refused to be that needy, weak person again. Because her parents had withheld love and affection, she'd craved attention and she'd looked for it in all the wrong places. It had taken her a long time to wake up and become emotionally independent but, since her midtwenties, she'd been too scared to test those sexual waters again.

What if those *I-think-I-might-love-him* and *does-he-like-me* and *I'll-do-anything-to-keep-him* feelings came roaring back again? It had taken her so long to find herself, to be at peace with who and what she was, that she couldn't take the risk of backsliding, of letting Hunt crawl under her skin and into her heart.

She couldn't, wouldn't, take the risk of reverting back to that scared, insecure person she'd been.

The combination of Christmas and Hunt could do that to her. No, she was right to refuse his offer of a quick affair.

But what if she slept with him and managed to stay emotionally detached? What if she trusted herself a bit more, trusted that the five years since her last broken heart had healed her? What if she was perfectly capable of handling a quick affair with Hunter? What if she was cured of her attention-seeking habit?

If that had happened, was she refusing Hunter for nothing? Was she missing out on some spectacular sex with Hunter for a no-longer-valid reason? If she was cured of her youthful folly, she could not only embark on a blistering affair with Hunter but she could also, when she returned to London, start to date again.

Was she making a huge mistake by simply assuming she was still weak?

"Adie."

Adie hauled in a deep breath, grateful oversized sunglasses covered her eyes because, damn, Hunt tempted her to rethink her no-sex stance. In designer jeans, desert boots and a gray-and-blue-flecked sweater worn under a battered bomber jacket, he looked relaxed and younger than usual. And she liked the thick stubble on his jaw and his messier-than-usual hair. Hair she wanted to run her hands through, hair she wanted to grip as he kissed his way down her stomach, over her hipbone…

"Hi."

"Hi back. Thanks for giving up your morning," Hunt told her, blowing on his hands.

His fantastic eyes searched her face. "Everything okay?" he asked.

No. Because every time I see you, I want to shed my clothes and seduce the hell out of you.

Adie pulled a fake smile onto her face. "Sure. Everything is fine." She stamped her feet. "Damn, this weather is ridiculous."

"Yeah, I wish I could blow off work and head for the islands," Hunt told her, placing his hand on her back and directing her to walk south. "Hot sand, pretty girls in bikinis, big surf."

Icy mojitos, warm water…bliss. "Do you surf?" Adie asked him.

Hunt nodded. "Whenever we could, Steve and I used to head to Hawaii to catch some waves. We'd spend our days surfing and our nights partying, drinking and chatting up girls."

Wanting to dig a little deeper, Adie tossed out another question. "You and Steve were pretty close, right?"

Hunt stared off into the distance and took a moment to respond.

"He was my best friend and my brother, in every way that counted. When I lost him, I felt…adrift. When you don't often connect with people, you treasure the people with whom you do experience that connection."

She'd tried to connect with everyone when she was younger. Hunt, it seemed, hadn't tried at all. Different people, different paths.

"Kate and I are relatively new friends, but I tell her more than I do most. Or maybe I end up telling her stuff because she won't let me keep any secrets," Adie admitted.

Hunt laughed. "Steve was like that, as well. He'd push and push until you eventually realized it was easier just to tell him. But he was a great secret keeper."

She trusted Kate, as well. "Were Kate and Steve very alike? I mean, I know they looked alike but were their personalities similar?"

"Peas in a pod," Hunt replied, dipping his hands into the pockets of his jacket and shortening his long stride so she didn't have to hustle to keep up with him. "Steve knew all my secrets and if you are not careful, Kate will soon know all yours."

She already did. Not that Adie had any great and dark secrets; her parents were selfish and being around them hadn't been fun. She worked too hard and because she'd been so in love with the idea of love, she no longer dated, especially at Christmas. She might be a workaholic but her life wasn't that complicated.

"Around this time of year, and after days like yesterday, I miss him the most."

Adie's step hitched at his unexpected statement and she darted a look at his face. Under his scruff, the muscle in his jaw was rigid with tension as were the cords in his strong neck. He also looked slightly paler than he had minutes before. Yeah, this was a very tough, touchy subject and Adie knew he wouldn't appreciate any sentimentality or trite expressions of understanding.

In fact, she was amazed they'd gone this deep, this quick. After all, Hunt kept telling her he didn't do emotional connections.

Adie felt the intense desire to comfort him, to wrap her arms around his waist and bury her face in his neck. Hunt, she was sure, wasn't familiar with the restorative powers of a hug, with how good it felt to lean on someone else.

Knowing she needed to take baby steps, Adie pushed her hand into the pocket of his jacket, sliding her fingers between his. She ignored the look of surprise he sent her and just squeezed his hand, hoping he understood that, just for this moment, he wasn't alone.

Hunt's hand tightened around hers and she laid her head on his shoulder, grateful for his big body sheltering her from the icy wind. Reminding herself that they were associates and not lovers, she reluctantly straightened and tugged her hand from his.

Hunt, however, refused to let her go.

Well, okay then.

Trying to ignore thoughts of how wonderful she felt snuggled up against him, she reminded herself they were just colleagues—even if they were holding hands—and asked him why he'd wanted her company this Sunday morning.

Hunt pulled a folded piece of paper out of his back pocket with his free hand and shook it open. He handed it to Adie and she scanned the typed notes.

"It's a list of names, denoting age and sex." She looked at Hunt and saw the hint of red blooming on his neck. Hunt was embarrassed? She didn't think he had it in him.

"An explanation, Sheridan?"

They approached a crossing and stopped behind a young couple pushing a toddler in a pram. Adie was about to tell him to hurry up with his explanation, but he gave her a small shake of his head. Frowning, she looked around and saw that his presence was gathering interest. The young father nudged his wife and mouthed "Hunter Sheridan," and another man surreptitiously pulled out his phone to snap a photo. The young mom and the other women standing around were content just to look at him, their eyes filled with female appreciation.

Adie couldn't blame them; he was eye candy.

Hunt took the paper from her, folded it up and placed it back into his pocket. Ignoring his admirers, he placed his hand in the middle of Adie's back to usher her across the road.

Adie turned around and looked back at the crossing and noticed that people were still watching. "I know that you are a Manhattan mover and shaker, but I didn't realize you were so recognizable."

"I played for, and now co-own and sponsor, one of the greatest baseball teams in the country," Hunt explained, "My face is out there."

And it didn't hurt that it was such a stunning face too.

"Yeah, all that ugliness is very memorable," Adie said, her tongue firmly in her cheek.

Hunt's hand moved up her back to squeeze the back of her neck. "Brat."

"I am," Adie cheerfully agreed. "And you still haven't told me about the list and why I am walking around Manhattan with you instead of drinking coffee in my pj's and thinking about breakfast."

"Yeah, that." Hunt twisted his lips. "It's a list of the kids currently in residence at a foster home situated in Albany..."

Hunt stopped talking and Adie knew that if she

pushed him, he might clam up or, worse, change his mind about this morning.

"Most of those kids will be spending Christmas there. Their foster mother is one of those amazing people who step up, every single time. The social workers know that when they are up against the wall, they can call Miss Mae, and she'll make a plan to take in another kid."

Adie had always admired people like Miss Mae. Not wanting to repeat what her parents put her through, and now that she was older and smarter, she couldn't imagine having kids of her own, never mind taking in kids who'd walked through several levels of hell already.

Hunt quietly continued his explanation. "I've been confidentially supporting the home for years, working through a social worker who deals with Miss Mae. Normally, I channel the funds through her and at this time of year, I give her extra money to buy presents for the kids and Miss Mae gets them what they need. But Miss Mae has been ill, and the social worker broke her foot so neither can get out to buy presents and I don't want the kids to go without."

"Surely there are other social workers, someone on your staff who could help you? Or, here's a novel idea, a concierge?"

Hunt pulled a face at her mild sarcasm. "I considered all those options, but it's really important to me that I keep this particular contribution under the radar. The only person, besides you, who knows what I am doing is the social worker. Secrecy is imperative."

Okay, Adie was now confused. "But you have a foundation, you give away money all the time. Why the need for secrecy?"

Hunt ran his hand over his face. "Ah, that. Well, because Miss Mae wouldn't accept it."

Adie jerked to a stop and faced him, puzzled. "I don't understand. Running a foster home has to *be* expensive and I'm pretty sure the state doesn't cover all the bills. Why wouldn't she accept your help?"

Hunt rubbed the back of his neck, obviously uncomfortable.

Adie wanted to tell him she didn't need an explanation but her curiosity kept her from forming the words. She wanted to know.

"Miss Mae was my foster mother and I lived with her for two years."

Oh, Hunter.

"Where were your parents?" Adie gently asked him, trying to keep her tone as conversational as possible. Pity, she knew, would make him retreat.

"My mom had quite severe mental health issues, she was in and out of psychiatric facilities."

"And your dad?"

Hunt shrugged. "He's just a name on my birth certificate."

Adie listened intently, knowing he was giving her a little insight into his past and his thinking. She felt…well…it was an old-fashioned word but…

honored fit the bill. Hunt, she was pretty sure, didn't often speak about his past.

And he still hadn't explained why he needed to secretly support Miss Mae. "Tell me about your highly classified mission," Adie said, lightening her tone to ease some of his tension, "and why Miss Mae won't take the help you seem to think she needs."

"Uh, that would be because, years and years ago, I waltzed into my old home full of sass and importance, with a truckload of stuff—furniture and appliances and clothes—and flung it at her, expecting her to throw her arms around me and tell me how wonderful I was. I hadn't seen her for a couple of years and wasn't very good at keeping in touch and she was already pissed at me for my silence.

"My intentions were good, but my enthusiasm ran into her pride. She lost it and ripped into me, told me that I was too arrogant by half, that she wasn't a charity case and she'd survived for a long time without my help. I yelled, she yelled. I called her ungrateful, she called me a patronizing brat…"

He shrugged. "I handled the situation badly but she has more pride than Lucifer."

So, she suspected, did Hunt.

"So now you support her quietly, through the social worker."

"Lauren tells me what she needs, I provide it. Quietly. That's why it can't go through the foundation, I don't want to risk her getting wind of who her benefactor is and getting all huffy again."

There was something so touching about a tough guy, hard and determined, with a soft center. Hunt came across as a driven, hard-as-nails business-man, but he hadn't forgotten where he came from or who helped him along the way. And, she might be wrong, but she suspected that Miss Mae was more of a mother figure to him than his own mother had been. The rift between them still seemed to have the power to scorch him.

And, if Miss Mae was as fond of Hunt as he was of her, she had to be hurting too.

"How long ago did this happen?"

Hunt wouldn't meet her eyes and Adie knew he didn't want to answer her question. "Hunter?"

"Twelve years ago," Hunter reluctantly admitted. When she stopped and just stared at him, he lifted his hands. "She's stubborn!"

"You haven't spoken to her in more than ten years?" Adie demanded, her voice rising.

"Oh, we've spoken, we're not that bad. We lunch every couple of months—at her favorite diner—and she always insists on paying for her half." Hunt scowled, obviously irritated. "But she won't hear of me paying for anything else because she promised me, over a decade ago, that she'd never take a cent from me. I've offered to buy her a bigger house and a new car but she keeps refusing."

"Wow, that's taking stubborn to a whole new level."

"Tell me about it," Hunt grumbled.

"Come on, she must know you are paying for the kids' Christmas presents," Adie protested.

"I'm sure she suspects, but since the social worker won't discuss the donation or tell her where it comes from, her pride will let her accept the help." Hunt looked frustrated. "Damn, she's a handful."

"But you love her."

Hunt's shrug was as much confirmation as she was going to get, but actions said so much more than words. It was obvious he absolutely adored Miss Mae.

"So, it looks like we are going to spend the morning buying Christmas presents for a bunch of kids," Adie said, tapping her foot on the sidewalk.

Relief softened Hunt's mouth and the tension in his body eased. "I'll pay you for your time, of course, but I'd like to keep this separate from the concierge business."

Please, she wasn't going to take payment, not for this.

Touched by his willingness to do what was right, Adie slowly nodded. "I am very happy to spend loads of your money and I'll even help you wrap the presents but it's going to cost you."

"I just said that I'd pay you," Hunt pointed out, but his mouth twitched at the corners, indicating his amusement. Funny how she was learning to read him.

Adie placed a hand on her stomach. "That's not the type of payment I was talking about..."

Humor touched Hunt's eyes. "What are you thinking? Flowers, dinner, a helicopter ride over Manhattan?" He flashed her that sexy half grin. "A night of unbridled passion?"

Adie rolled her eyes. "Nice try, Sheridan. Nope, you need to feed me. A girl can't shop on an empty stomach."

"That I can do," Hunt said, placing his hand on the small of her back and steering her down a narrow street. "I know a place where they serve the best bagels in the city. But feel free to change your mind. Especially about the night of passion."

"Don't tempt me, Sheridan," Adie muttered.

When Hunt laughed, Adie realized she'd spoken out loud. *No, Adie, don't even think about it!*

But how could she not?

Six

Hunt, in the middle of composing an email, felt the car stop. He lifted his head to look out the window. Pete had parked in his usual spot next to the portico of The Stellan and was leaving his seat to open the door for Hunt.

Hunt saved his work, closed the lid to his laptop and shoved it into his briefcase. He shook his head when his car door opened. Pete was in his seventies, it was cold enough to freeze nitrogen and the rain was turning to sleet, but despite telling him a hundred times that he was more than capable of opening his own car door, Pete was old school and refused to listen.

It had been a day from hell, Hunt thought, as he left the car and thanked Pete. The assistant Hunt was sharing with his CFO was out sick and he'd spent the day tracking documents and files, searching for emails and answering his own phone.

Hunt heard the ding of a message arriving on his phone and pulled it from the inside pocket of his jacket. Griselda? Now what?

If I sign all the releases and legal documents in the world, would you consider giving me your biological matter for me to use to get pregnant?

Hunt read the message, then read it again to make sense of her request. It sounded like Griselda wanted his sperm...

What the actual hell? Hunt didn't hesitate, his fingers quickly typing a reply.

That would be a hard no.

What was Griselda thinking? He didn't want kids, but there wasn't a chance in hell of him handing over his genes and not having any contact with his child afterward.

And really, if there were a test to prove their suitability as parents, Hunt doubted he and Griselda would pass.

Hunt didn't know a lot about raising children but he knew they needed love and affection and time. Neither he nor his ex had it in them to provide anything their offspring needed. He didn't know if he ever would. So why did the image of a little brown-eyed, dark-haired baby keep drifting in and out of his mind, a cute toddler sitting on Santa's lap, squealing at the sight of presents under the tree?

Those images didn't stop at babies and toddlers. He could also see himself spending hours in the batting cage with his son, walking his daughter down the aisle...

Hunt rubbed his hands over his face and cursed. What the hell was wrong with him? There had to be a logical explanation. Hunt pondered the problem and decided it had to be a combination of Christmas and viewing the storyboard earlier for the summer advertising campaign for Sheridan Sports featuring happy families engaging in sporting activities. He was overreacting, a natural response to facing what he didn't have, what he'd once desperately wanted.

He no longer wanted kids, didn't want a wife or a family to call his own. His work was all that was important, work he could control. Work, unlike his mother, wasn't a constant disappointment. Work, unlike his first wife, didn't betray you by spending all your money and sleeping around on you. Work couldn't die and leave you without your best friend.

Work was simple; relationships weren't.

Hunt sighed, conscious of a headache building at the back of his skull. All he wanted was a whiskey, a couple of hours of silence and some time to decompress. He couldn't wait to get up to his quiet, empty apartment and unwind. After a busy weekend and a long day of meetings, he was peopled out.

He needed space to breathe and to think.

That being said, he still, inexplicably, wanted to see Adie, to be with her. She hadn't come into the office today and he'd missed her, looking up eagerly every time someone knocked on his door. He'd then spent the next ten minutes feeling annoyed at his disappointment.

Despite wanting to be alone, he wouldn't mind seeing her wide smile, to look into her dark eyes, to hear her say…well, anything in her classy, British accent. Kissing would be great, taking her to bed would be friggin' fantastic, but he'd reluctantly settle for laying eyes on her.

Needing her, wanting her more than he needed solitude to decompress, irritated the hell out of him.

"Mr. Sheridan? Are you coming in?"

Hunt jerked at the sound of his doorman's voice and looked over his shoulder to see Glen holding open the door to his building.

Hunt strode inside, desperate for a drink and to slump back on his couch. He'd watch the city lights and try not to miss Adie or Steve and he'd make an attempt to relish his time alone. To banish those images of things he no longer wanted…

"Mr. Sheridan—"

Hunt ignored his doorman's call, waving his words away. Stepping into the private elevator that would take him directly to his penthouse, he slapped the button to close the door and saw Glen's shocked face.

"But I need to tell you—"

He'd had enough of people today and whatever Glen had to say could wait. Hunt rested the back of his head on the shiny metal skin of the door and closed his eyes. If he were normal, if he had any skill at relationships, he would be coming home after a crap day and stepping into the warm embrace of a partner, a wife, a significant other. She'd hug him, rub his back, pour him a whiskey and maybe take him to bed to distract him.

He wanted that tonight and for the person waiting for him to be Adie. He so wanted her to be standing in his space when the doors to the elevator slid open, seeing her wide smile and messy short hair.

Hunt shifted from foot to foot, annoyed that he kept pulling thoughts of her front and center. She was getting under his skin. In the middle of his meeting today, he remembered Adie having a long conversation about a skateboard with the hipster clerk at a famous surf and skate shop yesterday, asking him about the width of the deck and low, high and mid trucks. During a call to his accountant, he remembered her spending a half hour debating between two very lifelike, almost creepy-looking baby dolls, her face intense and animated.

She was fun to be around and he could do with her dry sense of humor and quick smile. He also wouldn't mind getting her naked.

Nope, he wouldn't mind that at all.

Hunt tapped the back of his head against the elevator wall, mentally and physically frustrated. Adie was someone who worked for him, someone who would be in Manhattan for only the next couple of weeks. He shouldn't be thinking about her, wishing she were here, missing her.

He never gave women, anyone, this much mental attention and it was time he stopped.

Hunt felt the elevator slow and then the doors soundlessly slid open. Music, hot and loud, assaulted his ears and his headache immediately intensified.

Stepping into the hallway, he dumped his briefcase onto the hall table and rubbed his fingers across his temple. This was an ultrasecure building and the only person who had unrestricted access was his cleaner. Since he'd caught Flora using his stereo system before—which he normally didn't mind—Hunt immediately assumed that her college classes had been switched and she was working late.

Exactly what he *didn't* need.

Thinking that he needed to kill the music before his head exploded, Hunt stepped into his living area and blinked. He closed his eyes and pushed his forefinger and thumb against his eyelids, hoping the mess would disappear, but when he opened them again, it was still there. His handcrafted, stainless steel and glass-top coffee table was pushed to the side and was piled high with ribbon and festive too-bright wrapping paper.

Sheets of it were scattered across the wildly rare and expensive navy-and-cream carpet made in the ancient city of Tabriz, and piles of presents, all wrapped, were scattered across the room.

Hunt stepped over a heap of Christmas presents for Mae's kids and picked up the universal remote buried in the detritus on the coffee table. He punched the power button and silence, welcome and warm, fell. Thank you, Jesus, he could finally think.

And God, what a mess. He hated chaos, physical and mental; it reminded him of his less-than-stable childhood, of sharing rooms with far too many boys, of not having any privacy, of feeling out of control.

This was his home and, obviously, Adie had come around sometime today, started on wrapping the presents for Miss Mae's foster kids and left, shutting the door on the disorder.

Not what he expected...

"Hunt? Is that you?"

Hunt turned at the feminine voice coming from the direction of the kitchen. His heart sighed with pleasure, irritating him further. He wanted to be alone, dammit.

Or he *should* want to be alone.

And how dare Adie think she had a right to be in his space when he got home, had a right to make a shamble of his very orderly and exquisitely deco-rated living area?

He heard movement behind him and Hunt's entire system sighed and settled in a silent, but potent, *there she is* as Adie walked into his living room, dressed in faded jeans and a thigh-length cream jersey, thick socks on her feet. She held a glass of wine and…

And she looked right.

She looked like she belonged.

And that terrified Hunt.

And because he was scared stupid at how right she felt in his life and in his space, he lashed out. Rationality be damned.

"What the hell are you doing?" he roared.

Adie's bright smile faded and she followed his eyes to the paper and presents on his floor.

"Uh—"

"You don't have any right to be here, messing up my place, making yourself at home!"

The glass in her hand wobbled and her complexion changed from warm cream to cold milk. Her eyes turned to burning coals and her lips thinned.

"You told me you'd be done by five!" He tapped the face of his watch. "It's after nine!"

"I know what time it is, Sheridan," Adie calmly replied, placing her wineglass on the wooden trunk that served as a side table for his long buffalo hide couch. Hunt strode over to her, picked up her glass and whipped a coaster under the foot to capture the condensation rolling off the glass. The trunks were also antique, made from rare wood and would be impossible to replace if they got water stained.

Adie raised her eyebrows at his actions but Hunt didn't care. He'd grown up with nothing so he protected and looked after what he had.

Resisting the urge to take a sip from her glass, he strode over to the drinks trolley in the corner and dumped a healthy amount of whiskey in a crystal tumbler. He noticed a dirty glass next to the decanter and irritation rose again. "You're drinking my wine *and* my whiskey? And could you have not taken your dirty glass to the kitchen?"

Adie folded her arms across her chest and the look she handed him was pure disdain. "Wow. Who spat in your cereal?"

Hunt gritted his teeth. "I've had a day from hell and all I wanted to do was to come home, zone out in my uncluttered, peaceful home and chill. But it looks like a war zone."

Adie walked over to his red leather chair and sat down on the edge, bending sideways to lift up a flat-soled, knee-high boot off the floor. She slipped her foot into the shoe and pulled up the zip. Before reaching for the other boot, she looked at him, her pale face annoyed. Annoyed? No, her eyes were blazing with banked fury and held a healthy dose of hurt.

Hunt felt a wave of remorse, a tide of humiliation breaking over his head, but he couldn't apologize.

"Well, all I wanted to do tonight was go with Kate to a gallery in Greenwich Village because one of my favorite artists is having a one-night exhibition. But because you needed these presents wrapped as soon as possible, I came over here after I finished work— my day was also tough, thank you very much!—to get it done."

Fair point.

"Did you or did you not tell me to come over at any time, that Glen would let me in?" Adie asked, her voice slicing through him.

He had. And maybe that was what Glen had been trying to tell him… He should've listened and he could've ignored this ugly scene.

"I've been here for four sodding hours. I have paper cuts and a backache. I put on some music because I was bored, had a glass of whiskey to take the edge off the fact that one of my new clients thought it was okay to ask me to organize her a boy toy for some extramarital entertainment when she reaches St. Bart's. After explaining to her that I am not a pimp, I then spent the next three hours wrapping these presents, thinking that you'd never, not in a million years, begrudge me a glass from the open bottle of wine in your fridge, while I debated what pizza to order!" She hadn't lifted the volume of her voice at all but he could tell her anger and temper levels were rising fast.

Zipping up her other boot, she picked up her over-sized scarf and wound it around her neck. Slinging her tote bag over her shoulder, she stomped into the hall and looked around in frustration.

"Where's the damned button to summon the lift?"

Lift? Right, that was what the English called an elevator. Before his brain could catch up and form his answer to her question, Adie was crossing the carpet toward him to snatch the remote out of his hand. Scanning the buttons, she saw the icon for the elevator and jabbed it, throwing the remote onto the sofa when she was done.

He'd messed up. Badly. God, how could he salvage this situation? "Adie—"

Hunt followed her into the hall and walked straight into the elevator, its doors open. "Don't you dare talk to me right now, Sheridan, I'm seriously cross at you and I don't want to say something I'll regret."

Hunt placed his hand on the door to keep it from closing. "Like what?"

"That you're selfish and rude and unappreciative. And though you are hotter than a trip around the sun, right now you are being a dick."

She was right, but he didn't know how to apologize or explain. That wasn't something he did. The only word he managed to form now was her name so he said it again. He wanted to tell her not to go, to pull her out of the richly decorated elevator and take her to bed. He wanted to lose himself in her, for her to lose herself in him.

"Back off, Sheridan!" Adie flicked his hand with her finger and because she caught him by surprise, he lifted his hand off the door and it immediately slid closed. Adie's furious and hurt face disappeared. Hunt rubbed the lower half of his face before linking his hands behind his head and cursing.

He'd thought he wanted to be alone, but he was wrong.

So wrong.

* * *

Adie, who'd been staying at Kate's Chelsea apartment, was ridiculously grateful Kate was in Boston, reconnecting with an old college friend. She'd left on the three o'clock flight and intended to catch the red-eye home. Or, as she'd informed Adie, if said friend had retained his college good looks, she might not be returning home at all.

Adie hoped for the latter, because she really, really needed to shore up her defenses and reassert her mind's control over her heart.

She paced Kate's lounge in men's style pajamas, a glass of red wine in her hand, conscious of her bruised heart banging away in her chest.

Hunt shouldn't have the power to hurt her, in any way. He was her client, a gateway to picking up more business in this closed-off, cliquey world. And she had the proof of that. Since she'd started working for Hunt, she'd had many inquiries from Manhattan A-listers for her concierge services. People she'd normally have to spend months, if not years, courting, were coming to her because Hunt had tossed some business her way.

He was her *client*...

But—ack!—he was more than that.

She'd genuinely started to believe that, despite the sexual tension between them, they'd become friends. She'd stupidly thought he not only wanted her, but he also liked her and respected her. His behavior tonight cast that in doubt.

She hadn't been friends with a man for a long time so she couldn't be sure of the whole man/woman friendship dynamic. But Hunt had told her a little about his life with Miss Mae, had opened up about his past. They'd had fun buying the kids' toys—although she frequently had to drag him away from the tech stuff—and she'd thoroughly enjoyed his company.

Judging by his ready laughter and relaxed attitude, she thought he'd enjoyed hers, as well.

That was why his actions tonight had been such a slap in the face. Especially when she'd been giving up her personal time to help him.

And, let's be honest here, the out-of-the-blue attack reminded her of her childhood, of being her mother's verbal punching bag, for being blamed for stuff that wasn't her fault. In her head, she heard her mom accusing Adie of ruining her marriage, telling her daughter that it was her fault her dad spent time with his mistresses and that carrying a baby ruined her mother's body.

Adie took a large sip of her wine and rested the glass bowl against her forehead. Was she mad at Hunt or was she mad at her mother?

Oh, she was always mad at Vivien, Baroness of Strathhope, but she was also really angry with Hunt.

And he deserved her anger.

So, she could either continue to pace the carpet and wonder if Hunt would apologize—probably not—or she could do something constructive with her time, like reading through today's emails, something she'd yet to tackle.

Action was always better than brooding so Adie flopped into the nearest chair and reached for the laptop sitting on the coffee table in front of her.

There were at least ten requests from clients for additions to their Christmas shopping lists, another client wanted her to have her Knightsbridge apartment decorated for Christmas and another wanted a meeting in January to discuss a fiftieth birthday present for her husband.

Adie, forcing herself not to think about Hunt, replied and sent an email to her assistant in London to help facilitate the requests.

Adie heard an incoming message on her phone and picked it up, grimacing when she saw the message from her boy-toy-seeking client.

I'm sorry, did I go too far?

That would be a yes…

Adie started to type a reply, a gentle suggestion that the woman consider working with another concierge company, when the intercom buzzed.

Thinking it was the pizza she ordered, Adie hit the button to open the downstairs door and looked around for her bag to pay the delivery man.

When the knock came on her door, Adie wrenched it open and in one practiced movement, reached for the pizza box and held out her other hand for him to take her money.

That's when she recognized that pale, pale pink button-down, the tanned skin between the open collar of his shirt, the geometric black-and-white pattern of the tie hanging below his open collar.

Adie raised her eyes and her heart took flight as she met Hunt's light, almost tender eyes.

"I met the pizza guy downstairs," he stated, lifting up the box.

"Thanks." Adie tucked the money into the top pocket of his coat and tried to tug the pizza box from his hand. "You can go now."

Hunt kept his grip on the box. "Aren't you going to share?"

Adie narrowed her eyes at him. "Are you going to apologize?"

Of course he wouldn't. Men in his wealthy and powerful position never did. She'd seen it over and over again, had experienced it…

The privileged and powerful could mess up but they expected people to either ignore their mistakes or to clean them up.

Adie had no intention of doing either.

"I'd prefer not to do it in the hallway, but if that's the only way I can get you to listen, I will."

Adie blinked at him, confused. "You will what?"

"Apologize," Hunt said, his tone terse. "Can I come in— Okay, the hell with it. I was a jerk, Adie and I'm sorry."

Wow, he'd actually done it. Holy Christmas cup-cakes. Adie tipped her head to the side. "Did that hurt?"

Hunt's mouth twitched. "A little."

"Pity, it should've hurt more since you behaved so badly." Adie stepped back into Kate's small hall-way and gestured him inside. Hunt, still carrying the pizza, walked from the hall into the kitchen and placed the box on the island in the center of the room. Then he turned to a cupboard and pulled out a glass. Gesturing to the open wine bottle on the counter, he lifted his chin. "May I?"

"Sure. Unlike some people, I'm happy to share my alcoholic beverages."

Hunt winced. "Yeah. That wasn't my finest mo-ment."

Hunt poured and sipped before turning to pull plates out of a cupboard. He also found flatware in the drawer under the counter. He knew Kate's apart-ment better than she did, and Adie commented on the fact.

"Steve and I shared this apartment over ten years ago," Hunt explained. "Steve bought it and Kate bought it from his estate."

Adie had not known that.

Hunt looked down at the pizza box, his hands gripping the counter. He eventually lifted his eyes to meet hers and Adie sucked in a hard breath at the turbulent emotion she saw rolling through all that ice and smoke.

"I had a shitty day and I was annoyed that I missed you today. I don't miss people, Adie."

Everything inside Adie warmed a couple of degrees at his terse admission. She'd missed him too, and she'd thought about him all day, wondering what he was doing. She'd spent thirty minutes talking herself out of heading for his office for a late afternoon catch-up session. There wasn't anything important she needed to discuss with him; she'd just wanted to see his face. Adie compromised by going to his apartment and she'd taken her time wrapping the presents they'd purchased, desperately hoping he'd come home before she was finished.

"I was trying to convince myself that I wanted to be alone and that I needed some time on my own. I also had a bitch of a headache. I walked into my apartment and there you were and I was both confused and so damn happy to see you and I didn't want to be either. So I got pissed.

"And then I shouted," he added on an embarrassed shrug.

"You did shout."

"I'm sorry," Hunt said, looking miserable. "You make me irrational."

It was the nicest, grumpiest compliment Adie had ever received and her internal temperature rose another degree or two. If he carried on this way she might spontaneously combust.

"I don't like the way you make me feel," Hunt admitted, his knuckles white as his grip on the counter tightened.

Adie picked up his half full glass of wine and took a sip. Despite knowing she shouldn't and that she was playing with fire, Adie asked the question anyway. "How do I make you feel, Hunter?"

"Confused, excited, out of control… So damn horny I don't know which way is up. Or if I'm even breathing."

Oh, God, so she wasn't the only one dealing with some wild emotions. It was such a relief to know that Hunt—unemotional and distant—also felt unsettled and unbalanced.

Adie took another sip of wine, conscious of his eyes drilling into her. Meeting his hot gaze, she saw the desire in his hot, stormy gray eyes and saw how fiercely he wanted her. Men had wanted her before—as a notch in their belt, as a conquest, out of mild attraction, as a way to pass time—but, with Hunt, she didn't feel like she was his way to alleviate boredom.

He wanted *her*.

Nobody else.

And she felt the same. She shouldn't, it was dangerous—but she did.

Don't do it, Adie, don't take the risk.

Because it was Christmas, she was feeling more vulnerable than usual and she didn't want to slide back into the bad habits of her youth. But, on the other hand, she wasn't the desperate girl she'd once been, she knew her faults and her weaknesses, she wouldn't allow herself to feel more for him, to confuse sex with love. She could do this, maybe she *had* to do this, to prove to herself she was stronger than she thought she was.

Maybe she should trust herself, after all. What harm would one night do? And maybe, if they were lucky, a night long on sex and light on sleep would burn this need out of their psyches.

They should give into it so they could get over it.

It made sense to her...

Still holding his glass of wine, Adie took his hand and told him to grab the bottle of wine.

Hunt gestured to the box of pizza. "I thought we were going to eat."

Adie lifted herself up onto her bare toes and brushed her mouth against his. "Later. Right now, I can think of something else I'd rather do. Can you?"

Hunt's thumb slid over her bottom lip and his eyes deepened to the color of wet concrete. "I can think of several things I'd rather do and all of them involve you getting naked."

Adie turned her head so she could nip the pad of his thumb. "Well then, what are you waiting for?"

Adie turned away, but Hunt tugged on her hand and she turned back to him, feeling a little exasperated. If he kept delaying, she'd start thinking and she might end up talking herself out of this...

"Are you sure?"

Yes, no...*yes*.

Definitely yes. Because, when she was seventy,

she didn't want to regret not having a Christmas caper with one of the hottest men she'd ever encountered. She wanted this one night and tomorrow she'd shore up her defenses and play it safe.

Tonight, she just wanted him.

"Yeah, I'm sure. Now, are you coming or not? Or do you still have a headache?"

Hunt's laughter was low and wicked, and oh-so-sexy. "Like I'd use that feeble excuse. As for coming, I intend to, but only after you are two or three ahead of me."

Adie grinned at his quick wit until she saw that, under the joke, he was very serious. Yowzer, two or three? Holy hell.

"I'll settle for just one, Sheridan."

"I won't," Hunt told her, placing his hands on her hips and lifting her so that her eyes were at the same height as his. "With my fingers and my tongue, then again when I'm deep inside you."

Adie swallowed, sighed and placed her mouth against his. She let him carry her to the bedroom, anxious to get started.

Seven

Sex was the last thing he'd expected tonight, but since he was a guy—a guy who'd fiercely wanted this woman from the moment he first laid eyes on her—he'd take it.

He wasn't an idiot.

Easily carrying Adie through to what used to be his bedroom, Hunt feasted on her mouth, relying on muscle memory to get them to where they wanted to be. Habit had him kicking the door closed and he allowed Adie to slide down his body to stand on the floor.

He cradled her lovely face in his hands, wondering if he should ask again if she was sure this was what she wanted. But he could see the desire in her eyes, the flush of excitement on her cheekbones, on her neck. Using one finger, he pulled the material of her collar away from her neck and saw her pink-tinged creamy skin. When she closed her eyes, obviously enjoying his touch, he swallowed down the need to reassure himself.

This was something they'd been heading toward for the past ten days, it was inevitable. And in the morning, they'd be as they were before...

She didn't want more, neither did he. She'd confessed to being the type who felt too deeply, who got carried away, but that was when she was younger. She was older now and he'd keep them on even ground—he never lost his head and he wouldn't start now.

They were colleagues, friends having sex, they didn't need to complicate the hell out of this situation.

Then why did he feel a little nervous, like he was taking a step off a high cliff into a churning pool of dark seawater? He'd had lots of sex before. He knew what he was doing...

But making love to Adie would be different. That unwelcome knowledge had him hesitating.

What price would he have to pay for indulging in his need for her? What would he lose? He didn't know and Hunt didn't like taking a risk without knowing all the possible outcomes.

Adie's small hand came up to hold his cheek. "Hunt? Everything okay?"

Hunt blinked and shook his head. He focused on

her suddenly hesitant expression. "Um, if you've changed your mind, that's okay. No hard feelings," she told him.

He hadn't changed his mind; he couldn't. "Only the world ending, and you telling me to stop, would make me walk away, sweetheart."

Relief jumped into her eyes. "Oh. Then why are you just standing there, not touching or kissing me?"

Now that was a damn good question and something he intended to rectify immediately.

Not having an answer, Hunt lowered his head to hers, tasting her lush, sexy lips. Adie arched her back and wound her arms around his neck, lifting her hips and moving closer to push her stomach into his erection.

Needing to taste her fully, needing everything, Hunt placed both hands on her breasts, immediately noticing how her nipples hardened in response. Finding them with his fingers, he took advantage of her sigh to push his tongue into her mouth, tasting the red wine she'd been drinking.

For a moment, the world stopped turning. They were the only two people on earth and their passion not only ignited but detonated, sending spikes of lust scampering along every neural pathway in his body.

He wanted her, more than he'd wanted anyone or anything before.

Needing to see her, wanting to know whether his imagination came anywhere close to reality, Hunt lifted her pajama top up and over her head and pushed her bottoms over her hips. The fabric pooled at her feet as Hunt looked down, sucking in a harsh breath at her gorgeous, naked body.

She was pale, but her skin was lush, as if she were covered in a layer of clotted cream. Her breasts were small but firm, her nipples the rich pink of a pomegranate. Her stomach was flat, her belly button delightful and the small patch of hair between her legs was darker than the hair on her head. Her long, shapely, runners' legs were a delight.

"Hunt, you're staring," Adie whispered, trying to tug her hands from his.

"That's because you are so worth staring at," Hunt roughly replied, "I suggest you get used to it because I could do it for—"

Biting off the word—the *forever* nearly slipped out—Hunt told her to turn around, and when she finally did, Hunt took in her slender back and her world-class ass.

Man, if he lasted two seconds after pushing into her it would be a friggin' miracle.

"I'd like to look at you too," Adie told him, sending him an impatient look over her shoulder.

If he got naked, he wouldn't be able to hold back. Besides, there was something incredibly sexy about being dressed while your lover was naked...

After toeing off his shoes and socks, Hunt pulled Adie so her back was to his front and crisscrossed his arms over her torso, his hands on her breasts. Needing to see her, wanting his eyes on hers, he dropped his arms to her waist and gently lifted her, walking her across the room to where a free-standing mirror stood in the corner of the room. Her head dropped back to rest against his collarbone and her eyes were on his hands, watching their reflections as he gently pinched her nipples, making them harder than before.

"Look at me, Adie."

Adie's eyes lifted and clashed with his, dark brown slamming into gray and Hunt felt his erection jump. Adie pushed her butt into him and he groaned, grinding himself against her. He'd wanted to take more time to explore her but one hand, by its own volition, skated over her stomach and he bent his legs so that he could push his hand between her legs to cup her mound.

"Open for me, sweetheart," Hunt commanded and Adie spread her legs. Hunt sighed when her feminine heat hit his hand. Sliding his fingers between her folds he smiled when her juices covered his fingers. So responsive… Moving up, he rubbed his index finger against her clitoris and Adie stiffened in his arms, her eyes growing wide.

Initially, he thought she didn't like his touch, but when she held his hand against her and lifted her hips, he released a soft laugh.

Yeah, she liked his touch. Very much.

"Hunt, God, this…"

Hunt touched his mouth to her neck, moved his lips across her skin to nip the ball of her shoulder. He removed his hand from between her legs and dragged his wet fingers across her stomach and up and over her nipple, making it glisten. "I can't wait to taste you, to be inside you. I can't wait to make you mine."

Adie's eyes were foggy with lust and she surprised him by picking up his hand and placing it back between her legs. "Touch me, Hunter."

He laughed, happy to oblige. Hunt watched as pleasure tinted her skin a deeper shade of pink. Needing to see every bit of her, needing for there not to be anything between them, he lifted her right foot onto the seat of the chair next to the mirror, exposing her to his gaze.

Hunt saw the momentary flash of embarrassment cross her face, but before it could take hold, he spoke in her ear. "Every inch of you is lovely. So feminine, so responsive. I knew it would be like this…"

"Like what?"

"Fan-freaking-tastic."

Hunt, needing to know more of her, pushed one finger into her hot channel, felt her clench around him and smiled. His thumb brushed her bundle of nerves and she pushed down on his fingers, wanting more. Hunt slid another finger into her and watched as her mouth opened, her breath coming in excited, shallow gasps. He knew she was close, knew that with a little pump, another flick, she'd fall apart in his arms.

Adie, insensible to anything but her rising pleasure, tried to push her fingers between his and her happy place, but Hunt took her hand away, holding it against her stomach. "Let me do this for you, Adie."

"Then do it!"

Bossy. Hunt, wanting to hide his smile at her impatience, dropped his head back to her neck. After a moment, he rested the side of his head against hers, their eyes clashing again in the mirror. "Kiss me, Adie."

Adie half turned, stood on her toes, and her mouth found his. Hunt nearly staggered at the passion he tasted, blown away by her need for him and what he could give her.

Her tongue pushed into his mouth and he let her take control of the kiss as he decimated her control down below. Bending his fingers, he found that special spot deep inside and tapped it while, at the same time, he increased the pressure on her clitoris. Adie arched her back and yanked her mouth off his, breathing heavily as she tensed in his arms.

He waited for a second, tapped and swiped again and she released a harsh cry as she contracted around his fingers, her body shaking as her orgasm hit her. Hunt pushed for more and she convulsed again, a deeper, longer spike than her initial orgasm.

Hunt held her as pleasure consumed her, enjoying the gasps and groans of a completely fulfilled woman.

It didn't matter that he was rock hard, feeling like he was about to rip open, he could wait, he *would* wait. This was about Adie and about what he could give her, how he could make her feel. About learning about her body and what made her fall apart.

Hunt watched as Adie came back to earth, her eyes foggy with pleasure and surprise. She allowed him to hold her weight, and Hunt knew he'd never seen anything sexier than Adie standing naked in his arms, slumped against him, his hand still between her legs, his other covering one breast.

She met his eyes and smiled softly. "Wow."

"Good?" he asked, even though he knew that it had been. It was in her eyes, reflected in the satisfied tilt to her lips.

"No, amazing." Adie yawned and lifted a hand to her mouth, her eyes widening with embarrassment.

"Tired?"

Adie nodded. "Sorry, I haven't been sleeping well lately."

"Me neither," Hunt told her, turning her around to face him. "And I'm afraid that tonight won't be any better."

Adie arched her eyebrows as her hands started to undo the buttons of his shirt. "Why, do you have other plans for us?"

"I promised you at least another two orgasms," Hunt reminded her, his fingers exploring her wonderfully round, smooth backside. "And I always, always keep my promises."

"Oh, well," Adie said on a happy sigh, "I can always sleep when I'm dead."

* * *

"Did your client really ask you to find her a boy toy?"

Adie, half-lying across Hunt, nodded. She was physically wiped and mentally wired. Moving was an impossibility and that was fine because Hunt was an exceedingly fine mattress...

Adie wanted to frown but didn't have the energy. "She did and I'm so disappointed in her. She knows my rules."

"Which are?"

"Well, obviously, I don't arrange people's sex lives... *Ick.* Also, even more obviously, drugs are out of the question."

Hunt's hand stroked her skin from her shoulder to hand and back up again. "Good to know since I'd hate to see you in orange."

"Animals are tricky too. I will arrange for the transport of a pet, accompanied by a human, provided I have proof that the dog has been bought from a breeder with exemplary credentials. My clients want only the best, so they normally deal only with decent breeders anyway, so that's not a problem." Adie traced patterns on his pec with the tip of her index finger. "I'll source dogs, cats and horses—I once had to find a client a polo pony for his son— but I won't deal in exotics, I learned that lesson very early on."

"What happened?" Hunt's voice rumbled over her.

"One of my very first clients wanted a capuchin

monkey. I felt uneasy about it, right from the beginning. I don't like the idea of primates being kept in captivity, I'm not a fan of animals in cages…"

"But?"

Adie wrinkled her nose, remembering the fear in the tiny primate's eyes. God, she still felt guilty. "I needed her money. She was my first client and as rich as Croesus. It was a choice between taking the commission or making rent that month. I found her a monkey but someone reported her to the RSPCA, the UK equivalent of your Humane Society. They visited my client and asked where the monkey came from. Apparently, the dealer I got it from was running a smuggling operation bringing exotics into the country."

"Damn."

"Yeah. The officer laid into me, rightly so, and gave me a huge wakeup call. The monkey was relocated to a zoo and is thriving. Since then I'm very, very careful with requests that involve animals."

"How long have you had your business?" Hunt asked, changing the subject.

"Since I was seventeen, eighteen?"

Hunt lifted his head to look down at her in surprise. "Really? That long?"

"Yeah, though obviously on a lot smaller scale. The seeds of the business were planted at school." Adie folded her arms across his chest and rested her chin on her fist. "My ridiculously wealthy parents, and I say that not to brag but to make a point, sent me to a very exclusive boarding school but frequently forgot to pay the fees. My mother wouldn't give me an allowance, I had to ask her every time I wanted something and since our relationship wasn't great and I was stubborn, I refused to ask her for a damn thing. So I found ways to earn my own cash. I ran a little shop, selling chocolate and energy drinks and odds and ends. Someone would mention they wanted pizza and I would order ten in, charging by the slice. I became known as their go-to girl, if they wanted something but were too lazy to look for it, I would find it, buy it and add a hefty markup for my trouble. They'd pay."

"Impressive." Adie wanted to roll around in the warmth and admiration in Hunt's eyes. "You're obviously a natural entrepreneur."

"Yeah, when I'm feeling generous, I can almost be grateful to my parents for pushing me into my career."

Hunt stroked her hair and pushed his fingers into her hair to massage her scalp. God, that felt fabulous. "I'm discerning a little bitterness. Why?"

Adie shrugged. "My parents shouldn't have procreated."

Hunt frowned. "Well, I disagree with that statement because you are here and lovely. But why do you say that?"

"I wasn't a welcome addition to their world. I am, apparently, the reason their marriage fell apart, why they fight, why my father has affairs. Children change the makeup of a relationship."

Hunt's hand on her hip tightened and she picked up the new tension in his long, hard body. "They told you this?"

"My mother mostly but my father didn't disagree with her."

"Holy shit. My mother had her issues, she was in and out of state psychiatric facilities all her life, but I never doubted her love for me."

"My mom doesn't love anyone but herself," Adie told him before waving her words away, "My parents are the reason why I was an attention hound for far too many years. Any attention was good because I received none from them."

Adie sat up and rolled away from Hunt. She sat on the edge of the bed, her back to him. "Why are we talking about this? Are you hungry? There's still pizza in the kitchen."

She stood up and pulled an oversized rugby shirt off the chair next to her bed. Slipping it over her head, she looked at Hunt, who was watching her through hooded eyes. He was utterly at ease in his nakedness and he had every right to be. Big arms, a ribbed stomach, strong muscled thighs and sexy, broad feet.

Maybe getting dressed wasn't such a good idea; pizza could wait. She wanted to run her hands down those legs, tongue her way over that washboard stomach, moving downward to his most intimate area…

Hunt waited until her eyes returned to his face before smiling at her. "I like what you are thinking but after two rounds of spectacular sex, I need pizza and a glass of wine and a little time to recover."

Adie blushed, shocked he could read her that easily. Rocking from foot to foot, she watched him roll to his feet and walk around the bed in the direction of the bathroom. But Hunt surprised her when he stopped in front of her and gently pulled her into his embrace. It felt like second nature to wrap her arms around his waist, to lay her cheek on his chest.

She felt his kiss in her hair, his broad hand raking her shirt up to rest his hand on her naked butt.

To Adie, it felt like Hunt had taken her apart sexually, exposed her and left her feeling vulnerable and off balance. But his hug put all those shattered pieces back together again. It was a physical promise of safety and acceptance.

She could've stood like that forever, soaking in his strength, leaning into him, feeling his tender lips in her hair, on her temple. It was, by a long way, the best hug she'd ever received and Adie wanted to stay there for the longest time...

Possibly forever.

You are doing it again, Adie, you are acting the way you used to. You are running into a deep pond instead of tiptoeing around the edge. Stop, right now!

She was not going to fall in love with him or start fantasizing about a future with him. Her stay in Manhattan was temporary. Hunt was a one-night stand and she would not let herself weave dreams around him.

She dealt only in reality these days, and all that was real was the attraction burning between them.

Hunt pulled back and Adie immediately allowed her arms to drop to her sides. "What's wrong, sweetheart?"

Adie wrenched a happy smile from somewhere deep inside and tossed it his way. "Nothing at all."

This was just sex and she wasn't about to repeat her old cycle of "sleep with him, immediately fall in love with him, get your heart broken."

She was older and better than that.

"So… I'm going to heat up the pizza, find some more wine."

You have to establish boundaries so just get it done. Because you know he can't stay the night.

Having him stay after such excellent sex, would be tempting her heart a little too much.

"And then we can say goodnight. It's been a long day."

Hunt frowned at her. "You're kicking me out?"

She couldn't wake up to his sleepy smile in the morning, didn't want to find herself under him, with him pushing into her while she was still dreamy and half asleep. Well, she did, but it was too much too soon. She needed to rebuild her barriers.

If she didn't put some mental and physical space between them, she might slip back into the destructive patterns of her teens and early twenties. And that was a risk she would not take.

Please don't insist on staying. I might not be able to say no. And while I'm stronger than I used to be, I don't want to test that strength.

Adie forced her lips into a cheeky grin. "I know you like to call the shots, Sheridan, but my bed, my rules," she told him, turning away.

Hunt's hand shot up to catch her wrist and Adie stopped, sighed and looked at him. Releasing his hold on her, he cupped her face in his hands, his lips drifting over her mouth in a devastatingly tender kiss. "Relax, Adie, it's all good. If you don't feel comfortable with me staying over, I'll leave. You might not realize this, but you hold the power here."

"I do?" Adie asked, surprised. She'd expected a lot more pushback.

Hunt stroked the line of her jaw. "Of course you do, you always did and always will. I'm not gonna lie, I want to do this again, as many times as we can before you leave the city, and to that end, I'd like to make love, sleep with you, wake up and start all over again.

"But if you need some time to wrap your head around what's happening between us, then I'll go home and try and get some sleep," Hunt added.

"Nothing is going on with us!" Adie squeaked. "This isn't going anywhere. This is just us having some fun in bed!"

Oh, God, how embarrassing it would be if he

thought she was falling for him, the most elusive man in Manhattan! That would be a disaster.

Hunt pulled back at her ferocious statement and lifted his hands as if to ward off an attack. "Adie, relax! I didn't mean to imply that either of us wanted something serious!"

"Then what did you mean?" Adie demanded, her heart thumping and her breath ragged.

"Look, you told me that you haven't had sex in a while—five years, you said? Maybe you need to work through what happened between us, I don't know, I'm just speculating here because I know that women think about sex differently than men do."

"And what do men think?" Adie sarcastically asked, eyebrows raised.

"Mostly that we're so damn grateful to have gotten some," Hunt replied. His easy grin doused what was left of her simmering temper. "While you do whatever you need to do tonight, on your own, know that I'll be lying awake thinking of you. Then I'll have to take a cold shower and then I still won't be able to sleep and then I'll be as irritated as hell at work—"

Adie laughed at his overexaggerated whine, realizing he was teasing. "Nice try, Sheridan, but you're still going home."

Hunt dropped a kiss on her lips and tapped her butt. "You're a tough cookie, kicking me out into the cold night."

She was just walking away from temptation-on-broad-feet. And because she was, she refused to think of Hunter Sheridan as anything more than a temporary fling, a bit of fun, a way to pass the time.

He was her Christmas fling and she would not, *would not*, fall in love with her sexy client.

And, what was obvious, he wouldn't let her fall in love with him either. Good thing.

But he was still, Adie decided, going home.

Because, really, there was no point in tempting Fate.

Adie, having done a final inspection of Hunt's apartment before his guests arrived for his much-anticipated Christmas tree–trimming cocktail party, dashed down his hallway and skidded into the master bedroom, whipping off her sweatshirt as she barreled across the room toward the en suite bathroom.

She was running late. After she punched the key-pad on the wall next to the door, the shower heads instantly responded and hot water and steam filled the huge shower enclosure. Adie knew she'd miss Hunt's luxurious bathroom when she returned to London. She would also miss his massive bed, the way everything in his apartment was controlled by an electronic tablet, the incredible views of Central Park...

Most of all she'd miss Hunt.

Adie stripped and, leaving her clothes on the floor, stepped into the sophisticated shower, sighing when the double-headed jets pounded her body with hot water. By mutual agreement, and because they were both aware that they were on limited time, Adie had all but moved into Hunt's apartment, wanting to spend as much time as she could with him before she flew back to London at the end of the week.

They'd been sleeping together for two weeks. Christmas Eve was a few days away and their time together was nearly over, but she didn't regret one moment she'd spent with Hunt. This had been the best three weeks of her life. In between joining the Williams family for a weekend of skiing in Vail, she and Hunt went ice skating at Rockefeller Center and window shopping down 5th Avenue, gently arguing about which store had the best Christmas windows.

They ate at little-known diners and Michelin-starred restaurants and they had, once or twice, appeared in the social columns, with the reporters speculating about whether his relationship with Griselda was over and whether the private concierge had captured Hunt's elusive heart.

No hearts were involved—she hadn't let hers out of its cage—but Adie's business brain couldn't help feeling pleased for the publicity as she received quite a few inquiries for her concierge services after those articles appeared online.

It was definitely starting to look like she could open a branch of Treasures and Tasks in Manhattan, and before she left, she needed to have a meeting with Kate to thrash out the details.

Although Adie was pretty sure Kate was on board, if she changed her mind Adie would pick and choose her New York–based clients carefully and manage their requests from London. Distance wasn't an issue; she had clients all over the world and could manage their needs from the moon, if necessary.

But presently, she had to get ready for Hunt's stupendously exclusive and very formal tree trimming party. Right now, the eight-foot tree in Hunt's living room was stringed with lights, and boxes of handblown glass ornaments, ones she'd purchased through her supplier in Poland, were resting in their velvet cases, waiting for the guests to hang them on the branches.

Having organized these types of parties before, Adie was fairly sure Hunt's guests, apart from one or two, wouldn't bother with the tree, they'd be far more interested in drinking, socializing and eating the canapés provided by the exceptionally expensive chef she'd hired for the evening.

She'd do the bulk of the decorating, either during the party or later.

Adie washed her body, wishing she could dry off, slip into a pair of soft jeans and a pretty sweater and socks and curl up in a comfy chair with a glass of wine. Or she wished that instead of entertaining strangers she didn't know, she could open the door to the Williams clan.

Instead of expensive ornaments and fancy food, they could order Chinese and sing along to Bing Crosby and Frank Sinatra as they argued about where to put a papier-mâché Santa or a string of tinsel. She wanted to watch Kate and her brothers argue, see the soft smiles Richard and Rachel exchanged, sneak into the kitchen to kiss Hunt senseless.

She wanted simple and meaningful, a Nativity scene and red candles and gaudy decorations. She wanted colorful rugs on his neutral couches, badly wrapped presents under the tree, greenery over the door frames, mistletoe hanging in every room.

She didn't want rich—she worked all day with rich—she wanted *normal*.

Adie placed her hands on the shower wall and looked down at the tiles beneath her feet, rolling her shoulders as the hot water loosened the tension in her neck. In a few minutes she'd climb out, dry off, and then she'd apply some makeup and slip into the sexy designer dress she'd picked up earlier in the day. Comprised of black Chantilly lace, beaded and embroidered, over a nude fabric, it was both sexy and demure, with its scalloped V neckline and A-line skirt. She loved it and she hoped Hunt would too.

But she'd still prefer to be dressed in jeans, drinking red wine, trying not to think of the call she'd taken earlier...

Think about something else, Adie.

Adie went over her mental to-do list, hoping she hadn't forgotten anything. A Dubai client wanted a last-minute gift from Tiffany, and she'd sent Kate to buy the bracelet he'd seen online, a complicated design featuring diamonds and sapphires and costing a little shy of half a million dollars. She'd received the photographs from the floral designer who'd decorated her client's Knightsbridge flat. He'd done a fantastic job. But the client wouldn't get to enjoy her festive house after all, because—after telling Adie that her payment had been processed—they'd changed their minds and wouldn't be visiting London this year.

She agreed with Adie's suggestion that the flowers and the exquisite tree be donated but Adie was furious that Gid had worked his butt off during an already busy season, to fit in her request to decorate the house only to have her clients change their minds at the last minute.

Sometimes her clients could be real jackasses.

Like most people, there were days when Adie hated her job, and today had been one of those days and Adie couldn't help but focus on the negative.

How many more private chefs would she organize for marriage proposals to later hear that the couple had split up just a few years later? How many more holidays would she organize that would not be enjoyed because her clients changed their minds? How many more diamond-and-sapphire bracelets would she buy and ship, how many would be worn?

But she was dancing around the real reason for her distress.

Her day had spiraled only after she received a request from her client, a German businesswoman, the CEO of a perfume company. The call had rocked her, and for the first time in a long time, she'd had no idea how to respond to her client's blithe, this-isn't-a-big-deal request.

Sadness overwhelmed her, and Adie placed her hand on her stomach, pushing the sensation away. She couldn't afford tears now, or to remember the past. Her childhood was over and she wasn't that neglected child, nor was she a lonely teen, looking for affection.

Change your thoughts, Adie. Now, immediately. Switch gears and focus on the positive.

She was a successful businesswoman having a brief affair with a gorgeous, smart guy. It was Christmastime, but she was managing the blues, her emotions and her expectations. Maybe she'd finally grown up and could handle a no-strings affair. And she deserved an extra pat on the back for doing it at Christmastime, when she was, historically, more likely to slip back into those destructive patterns of looking for love in all the wrong places.

And maybe that was why she felt so very comfortable with Hunt, relaxed about where they were and what they were sharing. They'd spoken about their pasts and their expectations and it was a relief to know that Hunt didn't do relationships. He was as anti-marriage, anti-commitment and anti-children as she was.

They were on the same page, reading from the same book. He liked her, loved her body and in a couple of days, he'd kiss her cheek, hug her goodbye and send her on her way.

There would be no tears or regrets. In time he'd become a pleasant memory.

And maybe Hunt was her gateway man, the one who would show her how to be with a guy without any expectations or projections. That she could have a sexual relationship with a guy and remain unaffected.

She'd handled herself, and Hunt, well, Adie decided. She'd thoroughly enjoyed his company and his lovemaking and she'd managed to ruthlessly shut down any dreamy thoughts or wacky ideas of having a long-distance relationship, or any kind of long-term relationship, with Hunt.

She liked him, adored his body, would miss him when she left—but she'd resisted falling in love with him.

Thank God.

Adie rubbed her eyes with the balls of her hands, wishing she could crawl into Hunt's big bed and go to sleep.

Despite her mental pep talk, she still felt a little overwhelmed and a lot tired. Christmas was always the most stressful time of year for her and she generally worked ridiculously long hours. She was not only working hard, but when she did finally collapse into bed, Hunt was always there.

And because she was on limited time with him, and because she couldn't resist him, she'd always spend a few hours tangling the sheets with him.

Adie released a huge yawn, closed her eyes and rested her forehead against the tiles. She just needed a little nap...

Eight

Adie heard footsteps and then the shower door opened. She groaned when Hunt's thumbs applied pressure to that spot at the base of her skull, enjoying the sweet, sweet pain of tension releasing. Reaching back, she tapped his bare thigh, murmuring a quick hi, and a "man, that feels so good."

Hunt dropped a kiss onto her shoulder before massaging her shoulder blades. "You looked sad earlier. Everything okay?"

How long had he been watching her? Adie wanted to look at him but his hands on her back, thumbs digging into her spine, kept her facing forward.

"Adie, is everything okay?"

Oh, right, he'd asked her a question. "Yeah, fine.

Just tired." Not wanting to lie, she added, "And a little pissed."

"Why?" Hunt asked, strong hands working her glutes.

"A client told me today that she was leaving for the Seychelles, and that her eight-year-old daughter was staying home with her nanny and housekeeper. Then she tells me that she supposes she should—her words not mine—buy the kid some presents." Adie snorted her displeasure. "Her daughter was such an afterthought. It was like she was making arrangements to kennel her dog. I guess it just struck a very big nerve."

"Tell me why?"

Adie turned to face him, placed her hands on her hips and lifted her shoulders to her ears. She had the brief thought that she was as naked as a newborn but immediately dismissed it, feeling completely at ease with Hunt because he'd told her, over and over again, how much he loved her body.

And, because she was sure they were friends as well as lovers, Adie felt comfortable enough with him to explain.

"To understand, you'll need a little backstory." Adie pushed her hair off her face. "When I was four, my mother left my dad and took me to Europe, where we moved from castle to villa to apartment, living off her trust fund and her friends' charity. My mom was vivacious and pretty and entertaining and people were always happy to have her. Me, not so much.

And, not wanting to piss off her hosts, my mother kept me hidden away from the action. She was there to party, to entertain and be entertained, so I rarely saw her. In fact, most of my childhood memories are of my mother's back, watching her walk away."

Hunt didn't speak, but his eyes radiated empathy. Empathy she could deal with, if she'd seen pity she would've stopped talking.

"My father demanded custody of me, mainly because he mistakenly thought it would anger and irritate her. He was shocked when my mom agreed, very quickly it had to be said, and I was shipped back to England. Not wanting to look after me himself—I'd disrupt his life too much—he decided I should stay with my grandmother, at Ashby Hall, the family seat."

"That must've been quite an upheaval."

"It wouldn't have been so bad if they'd allowed my nanny to come with me, but no, my grandmother said she'd look after me." Adie pulled her bottom lip between her teeth and bit down hard until Hunt tapped her lip with his finger and told her to stop it.

"There's more," Hunt stated.

There was.

"It turned out that my grandmother wasn't thrilled to have me. They hired me another nanny—she was okay—and my dad did come back to Wales occasionally, mostly on the weekends, to see me. But then he met the first of many mistresses and I was forgotten."

"Jesus, Adie."

"When I was eight, my grandmother died and my mother came back to Ashby Hall to live—she and my father never divorced—and that's when the blame game started… I was the reason why my dad never came home, the reason their marriage disintegrated. She should never have had me."

"If I ever meet your mother, I might just choke her," Hunt growled, his gray eyes incandescent with rage.

"You think that now, but within five minutes of meeting her, I guarantee she'll win you over. My mother is the most charming person you'll ever meet," Adie told him, placing her hands flat on his chest.

"Anyway, the reason why I'm telling you this is because you noticed I was sad and I am. Somewhere in Germany, there's a little girl who is feeling lonely and unwanted at Christmastime and, because I know how hurtful that can be, I want to choke the life out of her mother, my client."

"Don't work with her again," Hunt told her, frowning. "Drop her."

"I can't do that!" Adie protested.

"Sure you can…" Hunt's thumbs slid up and down her hipbone. "You're in demand, Adie and that means you can pick and choose your clients. You don't have to do everything for everybody. Choose the people you want to work for, hike your prices so you become even more exclusive and ditch the people you find annoying. Or offensive. Or who irritate you.

"Trust me, the more exclusive you become, the more in demand you'll be. Rich people like what we can't have," Hunt told her, bending his head to kiss the side of her neck. "And talking about wanting…"

How was he always able to make her feel better, to settle her? Hunt was able to push away the harsh memories and lighten her spirit. He was dangerous…

Hunt's finger skated over her lower lip and Adie glanced at his waterproof watch and winced. "You have guests arriving in forty minutes, Sheridan and I have to dress, do my hair and slap on some makeup."

"I've seen you dress in a hurry and know it will only take fifteen minutes," Hunt told her, moving his hand to her breast, his thumb gliding over her nipple. "There's plenty of time for what I want to do."

"And what's that?"

"Instead of telling you, let me show you."

Hunt tugged her out of the blast of water and sat down on the ledge spanning the width of the shower enclosure. Pulling her down so she straddled his thighs, he lifted his hand to her neck and pulled her head down to ravish her mouth. After a few minutes of intense, hot, skin-melting kisses, Hunt pulled back, his eyes dark with passion.

"I can't get enough of you. I think about you constantly, especially when I shouldn't," he muttered, sounding annoyed. "How the hell am I going to let you go?"

Adie, knowing it was the sex talking, knowing

nothing that was said when two people were naked was admissible later, didn't answer.

Instead, she touched her lips to his jaw, dragging her mouth over his two-day stubble, up to his ear to tug his earlobe between her teeth. Hunt replied by pulling her closer, lifting her so her mound was pressed against his thick erection. Adie couldn't help lifting her hips, sliding against him to create a little friction, sending ribbons of pleasure shooting through her system.

Hunt dipped his head to take her nipple into his mouth, his tongue rolling over her bud. He managed to walk that very fine line between pleasure and pain and Adie wanted more...

When she forgot to regulate her thoughts, sometimes she wanted everything: the good sex, the conversation, early morning coffee, making love as often as they wanted...

Now, who was letting the sex talk?

She'd been so good keeping her feelings out of it, she wouldn't slip now, not when she was so close to leaving with her heart intact...

She knew of one way to stop thinking of Hunt in terms of forever and that was to stop thinking at all. When Hunt was inside her, rocketing her away, she thought of nothing but the pleasure they shared, the thrill they gave each other.

Impatient with herself and with him, Adie wrapped her hand around his shaft. His low growl of approval ignited her nerve endings. Without giving him time to move, or even think, she positioned herself and sank down onto him, groaning as he filled and completed her.

Adie hooked her ankles behind his back, placed her hands on his shoulders and rocked, loving the feeling of his intimate flesh connecting with hers.

"We need a condom, honey."

But he felt so good and she didn't want to stop. But he was right; this was how babies were made. And God knew, a baby was exactly what she didn't need.

The image of a black-haired little girl with Hunt's gray eyes flashed on the big screen of her mind and Adie could smell her baby girl scent, feel her soft hair and was blinded by Hunt's smile on that pixie face. She could see the little girl, touch her, smell her...

Adie shuddered, causing desire to course through her.

Right now, she wanted Hunt's baby. She wanted Hunt. She wanted a lifetime of sex, of sleeping beside him, of arguing about whose turn it was to make coffee. She wanted everything.

No, she *didn't*.

She was confusing lust with love, intimacy with intercourse.

Adie felt a tremor pass over her again and she moved her eyes to Hunt's face and clocked his worried expression.

"You okay? You turned a little pale."

Adie nodded, needing to reassure herself as much as she needed to reassure him. "I'm fine. Really."

Hunt lifted his hips and she felt him grow bigger inside her, setting those exquisitely responsive nerve endings on fire. "God, Adie, you feel amazing. I'll grab a condom now. I just want to enjoy you a little more."

This was intimacy, Adie thought, this was the truth. Skin on skin, heat on heat. This was real.

Adie rode him gently, swept away by pleasure, riding a wave of need. When he demanded more, she increased her pace. She stared down into Hunt's eyes, knowing that she'd see his face in her dreams for the rest of her life. He was going to be the man she judged all other men against and she knew, without a shadow of a doubt, they would all fall short.

Hunt wasn't perfect, but he was perfect for her. He shouldn't be, but he was.

Hunt gripped her chin and forced her to look at him. "Stop thinking, Adie. Whatever keeps pulling your attention away can wait. Be here, be with me."

Adie nodded, wishing she could tell him that she was with him, that she always would be. But instead of speaking, she slammed her mouth to his, trying to pour all her regret, all her distorted, useless need for him into a kiss. Hunt's hard, strong arms wrapped around her and he surged to his feet. Adie moaned when he slipped out of her.

Hunt carried her out of the shower and, ignoring the still pounding water, walked out of the bathroom toward his California king, tossing her onto the smooth comforter. Adie scooted up the bed as

Hunt opened the drawer next to his side and pulled out a condom. He took the thin rubber from its covering and rolled it down his shaft.

Lowering himself to the bed, Hunt gently separated her thighs and looked down at her most secret spot. Instead of sliding inside, Hunt dropped his head to lick her, and then he licked her again.

Adie placed her forearm over her eyes, convinced she'd expire from an overload of pleasure. Hunt teased her with his tongue, with his fingers, lifting her up to where she was sure she'd come, only to take her to the edge and leave her hanging.

Finally, when she was sobbing, begging for release, Hunt pushed into her. She was so close she needed nothing more than his gentle command to come and she did, pulsing and shattering and flying and sobbing.

Adie was dimly aware of Hunt's hoarse cry, him calling her name, but all she could do was grip his shoulders as the world shattered, realigned and shattered again. This was the essence of pleasure, the origins of the cosmic bang. This was where light started, dreams were conceived and stars collided.

This was the majesty of the universe in action.

Nine

Hunt looked across his elegantly decorated apartment to where Adie stood by the Christmas tree, her head bent over the velvet-covered box containing Christmas ornaments. Deep in conversation with a tech giant's wife, Adie lifted an ornament to the light, her finger spinning the glass.

The bauble shimmered and sparkled. As did Adie.

Hunt sipped his whiskey, his attention on her and not on his guests. He couldn't believe that three weeks had passed so fast and that Christmas was just a few days away. Adie would be leaving soon and his apartment, and his life, would go back to normal…

If working fourteen-hour days, being empty of colorful conversation—being empty, period—could be called normal. He didn't want her to go. Yet he couldn't ask her to stay…

For the first time in his life, Hunt wasn't sure what he did, or didn't, want. He didn't want Adie to leave his life, but neither could he ask her to stay in it. He didn't want to stop sleeping with her, but how could they maintain a physical relationship when she was six thousand miles away?

He was in no-man's-land, not wanting to lose her but not prepared to love her either.

They'd had fun, Hunt thought, but nothing lasted forever. He had proof of that. For the first few weeks or months after his mom left the psychiatric hospital, she was a decent mom, but being strong wore her out. Her inner demons always made a reappearance and sent her scuttling back to where she felt safe and protected. And him back to a new foster family or group home.

His friendship with Steve had ended with a car accident and Hunt's marriage had burned hot and died as quickly. Nothing lasted forever…

Even if Adie was based in Manhattan, even if they gave it their best shot, it would eventually wither and die. It was how things happened and there were no exceptions to the rule.

But, crap, he wanted there to be.

He wanted to end every party he ever hosted or attended by taking her back to his bed, their bed, only to wake up with her curled up against him. He wanted to share showers and meals, space and time, conversation and children. His wealth and his world.

But if wishes were horses and all that…

He could wish up a storm, but those wishes didn't translate into anything concrete. Dreams and hopes and wishes were for people who were optimistic and a little foolish. Pragmatists like him—and Adie— knew that everything ended and some endings were more painful than others.

The end of his marriage had stung, mostly because he didn't like to fail. Steve's death eviscerated him, and Hunt never wanted to experience grief like that again.

But if he let himself love Adie, only to lose her, he'd never recover. So it was simple. He couldn't let this relationship continue and he most certainly would not allow himself to fall in love with her.

And if he did, he had no one but himself to blame.

He didn't know why he was even thinking about this because Adie had told him she had no intention of deepening their connection. She'd chased down love and affection as a young adult and she'd been disappointed time and time again. She was now emotionally and financially independent, of her parents and of a man, and she didn't need anyone else to make her happy or to give her life meaning.

Like him, she was just fine on her own.

In those quiet, early morning hours when his defenses were down and his heart spoke louder than his brain, watching her as she slept, if he had the odd thought of wanting to be the one who made her happy, forever, then that was his problem, not hers.

"You haven't taken your eyes off her for a moment."

Hunt turned his head to look at Kate and scowled. "If that was true then I would've face-planted a hundred times or more."

"Stop being so literal," Kate retorted, "you know what I mean."

Unfortunately, he did. And it was true, his eyes were constantly seeking Adie, needing to know where she was, and once he caught sight of her in that black lace dress, he fought the urge to kick out his guests and take her to bed.

Or leave the guests to their own devices and take her to bed. Either would work.

Kate thumping his biceps muscle broke into his fantasies around middle-of-a-party sex. "What?" he demanded.

"Sometimes I'm too damn smart for my own good. Or rather, your good."

"Meaning what?"

Kate snagged a full glass of champagne from a passing tray and stared at the pale yellow liquid for a long time before answering his question. "Look, it's not a secret that I never liked Griselda and when I met Adie, the first thought that popped into my head was that she'd be perfect for you. That's why I asked you to attend her Christmas market."

Hunt stared at her, trying to wrap his head around

Kate's words. And her matchmaking. "I thought you wanted to use me as a way to break into Manhattan society, to pick up some new clients."

Kate's snort was in direct contrast to her elegant red Vera Wang gown and the classy diamond-and-ruby hairpin in her blond hair. "I am the daughter of Richard and Rachel Williams, who have been part of that world since before I was born. I am stupidly rich and invited to all the best parties. I didn't need your help to pick up clients or for you to introduce her to potential clients, Hunter."

Wow, talk about being slapped back.

Kate smiled at him. "Don't get me wrong, my connection with you doesn't hurt and Adie working for you has definitely impressed a lot of people, but neither of us needed you to establish her business."

Hunt sipped his whiskey and narrowed his eyes at Kate's smirking expression. "Okay, got it. Message received. Can we talk about your matchmaking scheme now?"

Kate slipped her hand into the crook of his arm and rested her head on his biceps as they both watched Adie. "I thought you were well matched but I never expected you two to have such hectic chemistry and be so well suited.

"I see you two together and you gel. You are both so close, this close," Kate lifted her hand, a tiny gap between her thumb and index finger, "to falling in love."

Hunt stepped back and folded his arms across his chest. "How much champagne have you had?"

Kate ignored his question, her eyes going back to Adie. "But I'm scared for her, Hunt. Hell, I'm scared for both of you. I know her better now and, while I don't want either of you hurt, I do know how resilient you are. You're a survivor, you can cope with anything, but Adie isn't as strong. She's worked so hard to become who she is today. If she falls for you and you don't fall for her back, it'll hurt her, Hunt.

"For Adie, love has been…elusive. If you don't plan on keeping her forever then you need to end it, Hunt, before she falls deeper and can't get herself out."

Hunt couldn't speak. He could hardly breathe. He wanted to argue with Kate, tell her she was allowing her imagination to run away with her, but he couldn't utter the lie. Kate, as observant as ever, had hit the nail on its head and demolished it in the process.

He either had to go all in with Adie or end it. And since he didn't want a relationship, didn't want more than what they had, couldn't deal with more, that meant cutting ties…now, immediately.

Well, as soon as possible. His skin prickled and ice invaded his veins. No, it was too soon. He hadn't had enough of her yet.

They had three days left together. They could be together during the remainder of her stay in the city and then they'd say goodbye.

"She's leaving in three days, Kate. Nothing much

can happen in so short a time." Was he trying to convince Kate or himself?

Kate didn't even try to hide her enormous eye roll.

"It's the most romantic time of the year, Sheridan!" Kate gestured to his window and Hunt noticed gently falling snow and the way it covered his balcony in a pretty layer of white. "This is the season of magic and miracles and, let's be honest here, stupidity! Babies are made, proposals are issued, I-love-yous seem to fall more easily. Don't get caught up in the hype, Hunter!"

"Have you ever known me to be unduly influenced, Kate?"

"Well, no," Kate admitted, a stubborn look on her face. "But there's a first time for everything."

Hunt rubbed her arm. "Relax, Katie, Adie and I know what we are doing. We're adults and very much have this under control."

Kate stared at him for the longest time and Hunt resisted the urge to squirm. Maybe this situation with Adie was a little out of control, but he intended to rectify that, to make sure they kept their intense chemistry corralled. He had no intention of getting hurt, but he could handle it if he did—Kate was right, he was a survivor—but he had no intention of allowing Adie to be affected in any way, at all.

Adie in pain was simply not an option. And if calling this quits three days before its expiration date meant avoiding that scenario, then that was what he'd do.

But in the morning, after he'd spent the night making love to her.

He'd give them both one last, glorious night to remember.

The next morning Adie opened her eyes to see big fluffy snowflakes floating to the ground as they passed Hunt's floor-to-ceiling bedroom windows. If she sat up, she knew she'd see the tops of the trees in Central Park dusted in powdered sugar, and Adie couldn't wait to find out if the busy city was the picturesque fairy-tale location she imagined it to be.

But for now, she was content to lie here in Hunt's huge bed, her bottom to his crotch, his big arm holding her close, his breath on the back of her neck, his big hand covering her breast.

Romantic, easy, lovely…yes, this was the perfect way to start a day.

Adie felt Hunt's hard erection pressing against her and heat rocketed through her. Why were they sleeping? They had only a few days left together, hours really, and they were wasting time when they could be making love. Rolling over onto her back, Adie turned her head to look at him and sucked in a harsh breath at the blazing heat in his eyes, the desire on his face.

She fell, and fell some more, unable to believe that such a masculine man could want her so much.

Adie tried to say good-morning but the words died in her throat, overwhelmed by the hot emotions she could see in his eyes. Yeah, tenderness was there, as was lust and was that regret? Or fear?

She didn't know; she couldn't tell. Neither could she ask. She simply wasn't ready for a heart-to-heart conversation.

Besides, she didn't want to talk, she wanted to feel, to be, to love this amazing, sexy man as the snow fell behind them.

Gently pushing Hunt onto his back, Adie straddled his thighs, dragging her wet core over his ready-to-play erection. He felt so good, so intensely hard and hot, satin over iron. How was she supposed to give this up? How was she supposed to walk away from so much pleasure, from how he made her feel?

You can't think about that, Adie, not now—all you can do is enjoy him. Take the moment, the hour, the day...and mentally record every memory.

Adie, not wanting to end this before it started, leaned down to kiss Hunt, her tongue sliding into his mouth. Holding his face in both her hands, she stroked her thumbs over his cheekbones, her fingers over his jaw, trying to imprint these feelings into her psyche, hoping to burn the way he felt and smelled, the way he kissed and tasted, into her subconscious.

Hunt's hands moved up and down her back, over her butt, up her sides, and onto her breasts. His touch, like hers, was a little desperate, as if he were trying to commit her to memory, as well.

Hunt gripped the back of her head, fusing her mouth against his, taking the kiss deeper and then deeper still. His need for her fed her own desire and she tilted her hips, needing more, needing everything. She felt rather than heard his moan of approval and her hands streaked over his upper body, trying to touch him wherever she could. Oh, how she wished she could completely fuse their bodies together. Having him inside her wasn't enough—she wanted more…

And once she got it, she suspected it still wouldn't be enough.

Hunt, his hand in her hair, tugged her head back and when she looked into his eyes, she gasped at the passion and need in his eyes.

"Goddammit, you're exquisite." Tightening his arm around her waist, he flipped her over and entered her with one long, sure, perfect stroke. Adie's legs encircled his hips and she pushed her nails into his firm butt, groaning with approval as he sought her mouth, his tongue dancing with hers.

For the longest time, Hunt was content to stay inside her, kissing her with a ferociousness he'd never displayed before. Without leaving her, he kissed her throat, pushed her breasts up so her nipples could meet his mouth, nibbled her collarbone but always, always returning to her mouth.

Pleasure dipped and peaked but Adie didn't want to come. She didn't want this to end. And Hunt didn't hurry them along, seemingly content to make their encounter last, to drag out this experience for as long as possible.

Because they'd never do this again…

The thought hit her—a hot, hard, devastating swipe. This was it, as soon as they were done— probably after they'd had a shower and cleaned up— he'd call it quits.

And that was okay; she knew it had to end. And if he didn't end it, she would. She had to. Sure, she was supposed to stay only another three days, but her feelings for Hunt were growing at warp speed— when had that happened? She'd been so in control! And by the weekend she might be thinking about forever, about marriage and babies.

No, she couldn't let that happen. She needed to pack up her stuff and *go*.

There wouldn't be any promises to keep in touch, to see each other again…her fairy tale in New York was over and it was time for her to return to real life.

Because if she stayed, if they continued this, they would start saying words they didn't really mean, I-love-yous and I-can't-live-without-yous.

No, it was better to leave while they liked each other, while Hunt still liked her. She wanted Hunt to have only good memories of her.

"Stop thinking," Hunt told her. "Be with me."

Adie wanted to keep some semblance of control but Hunt's mouth was demanding. His hands were insistent and he was driving his cock deeper into her, demanding her response. Her nipples tingled, her skin flushed and her channel pulsed with need as she hovered on the edge of an earth-shattering climax.

How could she feel so good but so miserable at the same time? How could she be two people simultaneously, one begging him to push her over the edge, the other silently screaming that she had to leave, that she needed to protect herself, that her bourgeoning feelings for him scared the skin off her?

Then her orgasm hit, crashing over her head and she begged Hunt for more. He responded, shoving his hand between them to find her nub while his hips pistoned into her. Adie felt herself rocket upward and when she felt his release, she fell over that cliff again, falling, falling…exploding.

Tears streamed from her eyes and she tasted them on her lips, confused and upset and throbbing with the aftermath of concentrated pleasure.

He'd made her fly, sent her to the stars and back, but now reality was rushing up to meet her, cold and hard and oh-so-unwelcome.

He didn't love her and this had to end.

Maybe he loved her a little and this didn't have to end.

No, he knew he loved her. No way did he want this to end.

Hunt, running across Bow Bridge in Central Park, skidded to a stop and slapped his hands on his hips. His breath made a circle of mist in front of his face. He ignored the freezing wind plastering his running top to his chest.

What he knew for sure, deep down in that place

where truth lived, was that he most certainly didn't want her to leave.

He'd thought he did, at the party last night he'd even resolved to break things off with her but thinking was easy. Doing, as he'd discovered, was impossible. His mind, determined to keep him safe, was convinced he needed to remain emotionally isolated and solitary.

His heart and soul, and body, couldn't conceive of a life without her in it.

Hunt placed his gloved hands on the edge of the cast-iron bridge and stared down at the frigid waters of the Lake. He'd vowed not to fall in love again, to have any emotional attachments, but Adie had snuck under his defenses and flipped that resolve on its head. He was scared of getting hurt, of course he was. He was terrified of losing her, but living his life without her scared him more.

He couldn't—he wouldn't—go back to the life he'd had before, an empty apartment, meaningless sex, his hours spent on work and more work.

He wanted something different, something meaningful...

And he wanted everything he could have with Adie.

He wanted that huge wedding, or a small wedding—whatever she preferred. He wanted to see her walking down the aisle toward him. He wanted to come home to her every day and wake up to her every morning. He wanted to see her rounded with a child—*his child*—to be there when she pushed a new life into the world.

She could be on her way to pregnancy right now. He hadn't remembered to use a condom this morning. But instead of feeling panicked and anxious at the idea, Hunt smiled, completely at ease with the notion.

His eyes drifted over the snow-covered landscape of his favorite park, and he could imagine a little boy with brown eyes playing in the snow, making tiny snowballs and throwing them at him, missing him by a mile. Or, if he inherited Hunt's pitcher's arm, snowballs that hit him square in the face. He could see his son's momma, another baby in a sling against her chest, the cold turning her cheeks pink, brown eyes sparkling with laughter.

It was easy to imagine his little family coming home to hot chocolate and coffee, Adie stepping over toys and books as she sank to the couch to lift up her shirt to feed their baby girl. He'd make them lunch, bathe the kids, then take his wife to bed and make love to her before one of the kids interrupted their sleep...

He suddenly and desperately wanted what Richard and Rachel had—a solid marriage, a lifetime of memories, children and companionship. Oh, he knew it wouldn't be easy—having tons of money wasn't a bulletproof shield against heartache, Steve's death being a case in point—but Hunt and Adie could work their way through it, love their way through it. They just had to stand together, shoulder to shoulder and face whatever came their way. They had to believe that love could conquer anything.

Hunt shook his head. He sounded like a greeting card, but it didn't make the emotion any less true. He'd sublimated his earliest dreams, pushed away his wish for a family because he'd been scared to feel loss and pain again, but a family was still what he wanted. And Adie was central to the family he imagined.

He'd never felt this way about Joni. Their relationship had been built on ego and pride. And his relationship with Griselda had been all about convenience. And, possibly, laziness. The thought of raising a child with Griselda now made him shudder. He and Adie wouldn't have separate apartments or nannies. He would be an active participant in raising their children. He'd take his son to the batting cages and little league practices, his daughter to ballet or cello lessons. Or, hell, vice versa if that was how his kids rolled. He'd be there.

Although he felt unsure and uncertain, he couldn't wait to dive in, knowing that he and Adie could do it all, together.

The only problem, Hunt thought as he started to jog back home, was convincing her.

Adie zipped her suitcase, grabbed the handle and pulled it off Hunt's bed. It hit the laminated flooring with a hard thump, narrowly missing her toe.

Her eyes blurry with tears, Adie looked around his chocolate-and-aqua room, wondering how she'd find the willpower to pick up her bag and leave.

But she had to…

Because she was sliding into love, doing exactly what she'd promised herself she wouldn't do. So she had to leave while she still could, while she had the strength to walk away.

Hunt didn't want this either, Adie reminded herself. He hadn't offered her anything or suggested she stay in New York or asked her to delay her trip and spend Christmas with him. But something was different, something had happened between them last night and earlier this morning. They hadn't just had sex—they'd made love.

Sex was easy, but lately, she and Hunt hadn't engaged in the biomechanical act. No, they'd made love, dammit, in every sense of the words.

Using their bodies, he'd pulled her into his mind and him into hers. There was a shocking intimacy in the way they touched each other that went beyond the prosaic act, it was as if Hunt knew her, could see inside her. They'd *connected*.

But she had to sever that connection, now, immediately.

Because if she didn't, if she allowed this to grow, there were only two possible outcomes. She'd start weaving fantasies around him and he'd soon become frustrated with her and call it quits. Or, if for some weird reason his feelings grew faster than hers and he wanted something permanent from her, she'd run.

Adie wrapped her arms around her waist and walked over to the big window, looking down at the snow-covered streets and trees. She would not do that to Hunt, would not allow him to think they had a future when she knew she was the ultimate runaway lover.

It didn't matter that Hunt had said he wasn't into commitment, that he was as anti-relationships as she was. She'd seen something in his eyes last night and it had scared her. Whether she was right or wrong, whether he was falling for her or not, it didn't matter, she was bailing before this situation got more complicated, before their feelings strolled into the party and ruined everything.

But damn, if there was one guy in the world who could tempt her to stay, persuade her to take a chance, then Hunt Sheridan was that guy, the only guy...

"Coffee?"

Adie furiously blinked away tears—she would not let him see her cry!—and hauled in a deep breath, testing a smile. She slowly turned to see him standing in the doorway, the two cups dwarfed by his big hands. Hands that had held her, stroked her for the last time.

It's better this way, dammit! You're walking away with your heart, without silly expectations, having had three weeks of the best fun, in bed and out of it.

And Hunt, Adie fiercely reminded herself, didn't "do" love. He wanted freedom, to remain unentangled, to give all his focus to his work. And that was why his relationship with Griselda had lasted for so long. She'd made no demands on him and had been happy to take as little as he offered.

Oh, God, maybe he'd restart whatever he and Griselda had...

The thought made Adie want to throw up. But it made sense—Griselda lived in the city, she made no demands on him and their whatever-they-had had worked for a long time.

Hunt stopped in the doorway to his bedroom and Adie looked at him, wishing she could freeze time. He was still dressed in his running gear and expensive sneakers. His solid black running pants molded to his muscular legs. He'd ditched his parka, but his light blue running top skated over his broad shoulders and over his wide chest to fall in a straight line over his stomach. His hair looked messier than usual and she knew her fingers running through those silky strands had contributed to his tousled look.

Despite his lack of sleep, he looked fit and healthy, and yeah, so sexy he stripped her of her breath. Hunt wasn't conventionally handsome but had the masculine face that made a woman look, and then look again. From this moment on, heavy stubble, hair the color of burnt sugar and gray eyes would always be her favorite color combination...

Hunt walked across his bedroom and placed

Adie's cup on the bedside table closest to her. Moving closer to the window, he pushed his shoulder into the glass, staring down at the park he'd just run through, the trails now slick with sleet.

"I see you're all packed," Hunt quietly commented and Adie searched his face, and his words, for subtext. She found none.

"Yeah, I thought I should go."

"Want to explain why? I thought you were flying tomorrow."

"I was, am." Adie twisted her hands together. "I thought that we should, you know…"

"I really don't," Hunt said, after sipping his coffee.

The "end this" stuck in her throat, she couldn't make herself say the words. Adie rocked on her heels. God, she hated this part. Saying goodbye was never fun.

"When do you think you'll come back to the city?" Hunt asked.

"I have to be back sometime in the New Year," Adie replied, her hands wrapped around her mug as if she were looking for warmth. "Kate and I plan on opening up a Treasures and Tasks by the end of February. Once the legalities are in place, I'll leave Kate to run the Manhattan branch and I'll only be making the trip back every six months or so."

"Since you have yet to mention contacting me, I presume that's not in the cards?" Hunt asked, his tone low and hard.

Adie forced herself to say the words. "No, I won't be contacting you."

"Would you like to clarify why? I thought we enjoyed each other."

Adie shifted from foot to foot and told herself to stop fidgeting. "We did—I did."

Hunt raised his eyebrows above suddenly icy eyes. "Care to explain, Adie?"

No, not really. It hardly made sense to her…

"I just think we've run out of road."

"Bullshit," Hunt snapped. "Tell me the truth."

Adie put her coffee down, jammed her hands into the back pockets of her tight-fitting jeans and lifted her shoulders to up around her ears. She went for the most valid, easiest-to-explain response. "I live in London, Hunt, you live here. Neither of us wants anything permanent so I'm easing my way out of your life."

"Easing? You're full-out galloping!"

Well, yeah. But he wasn't supposed to have picked up on that.

Adie forced a smile onto her lips and attempted to look jaunty. "Once I'm out of the picture, I'm sure Griselda will be very happy to take up where you left off."

Hunt's eyes flashed with anger and Adie grimaced. God, why did she have to bring up his ex? Oh, maybe because she wanted to know whether he intended to reinitiate contact with the blond ballet dancer.

Hunt stared at her, his expression suggesting she'd grown two heads. "Do you really think I'd go back to her? After what you and I shared?"

"We shared your bed, Hunt. That's about it."

"I thought we enjoyed each other as much out of the bedroom as we did inside it," Hunt replied.

And what did he mean by that?

"I'm only going to say this once… Griselda will never be a part of my life again," Hunt said, his words clipped. "We're done. She wanted something I couldn't give her."

Adie cocked her head to the side. "Love? Commitment? A proper relationship?"

"No, Griselda didn't want that from me. What she wanted was for us to co-raise a child together," Hunt explained, keeping his eyes on hers. "I told her no."

Holy hell, really? "And why didn't you tell me this before?"

Hunt's eyes narrowed. "Maybe because we were only sharing a bed, Adie."

Oooh, touché.

Despite knowing that she was dragging out this goodbye, Adie wanted to know more. "Did you say no because you don't want to be a dad?"

He was anti-commitment, anti-relationships, so his not wanting to father a child, to tie himself to a woman through a baby for the rest of his life, made sense.

Hunt held her eyes, his expression enigmatic. "I

didn't think I did. I've changed my mind about quite a few things since you dropped into my life, Adie.

"I don't want a cold relationship, Adie, with a cold woman. I don't want a nanny to raise my child, to visit my child in the apartment downstairs. I want my child to run down the hall and climb onto our bed, snuggled down between us, nag us to get up because he wants to play. I want to do the midnight feedings and bath times, read stories to our kids, take them to their sports games and ballet lessons and play in the snow. I want to be a dad, not their sperm donor or bank manager.

"Be my unborn kid's mom, Adie," Hunt added.

"What?"

Had he lost his freaking mind?

Adie looked at him, looking for the hint of humor that would tell her he was joking. But she didn't find it.

What was happening here? Instead of going up one level—let's try and keep this alive, let's see where this goes—he'd skipped five or six and went straight to the highest floor, the scariest level.

The urge to fling herself into his arms, to plaster her mouth against his and utter a series of yes's in-between kissing him senseless, was strong. Because joy flooded her system and her heart took flight, she forced herself to take a step back and hold up her hand. God help her, she needed to leave before she threw caution to the wind and said something stupid.

Like yes.

"I—I… Hunt, God. Where is this coming from?" Adie demanded, her voice turning shrill. "We've known each for three weeks and now you're asking me to be your baby mama? This was just supposed to be a three-week fling, Sheridan! No commitments, no strings, a good time and then we walk away. What the hell are you doing?"

"I'm trying to keep you in my life, dammit!"

"Why?" Adie shouted back.

"Because what we have is amazing. Because this can be something special, a once-in-a-lifetime thing!"

His words bounced off his walls, off the glass of his expansive windows and Adie felt them pummel her skin. Oh, no, no, no, no! She didn't want this intensity, hadn't asked for it, couldn't trust it. This level was way out of her comfort zone.

He hadn't mentioned the *L* word, but it was there, hovering between them. But love, expressed or not, would die. It always did. Maybe not by his hand but in time, by hers. She couldn't be loved, didn't want to be…

Love was a myth. Wasn't it?

Adie stared into his eyes, saw the tenderness under his frustration and felt herself leaning toward him, wanting to believe that this was it, that love could last, that she could change. But that wasn't fair, not to him and not to her.

She saw his face soften, watched as his hands

reached for her, but before they could physically connect, she jerked back.

She couldn't allow herself to be sucked into a relationship, a relationship that had no chance of lasting.

One of them had to be sensible.

"This is unrealistic thinking, Hunter, it really is. We've had a nice time but, deep down, you know we are both too screwed up to have the big house, kids and white picket fence. I'm the product of two of the most dysfunctional people in the world and you, when you recover from this rush of blood to your brain, you'll regret your words. In time you'll feel frustrated at having to balance a girlfriend and your work. You'll start to resent me and I'll start to hate you and if we have a kid together, it'll be a hundred times worse. And we'll screw up a child who didn't ask for any of this. You haven't thought this through."

"I'm thirty-five years old Adie, and I run a multibillion dollar company. I know my own mind," Hunt said, sounding annoyed. He reached out to take her hand and sighed when Adie hid her hands behind her back. She couldn't let him touch her. If she did, she'd sink into him and that would be disastrous.

"Give it a shot, Adie. Give us a chance. I know we live in different cities, but we'll figure it out. We'll take it step by step if that makes you feel more comfortable."

Adie shook her head, walked over to the bed and picked up her bag, slinging it over her shoulder. Then she grabbed the handle of her suitcase and tipped it onto its wheels. "I can't, Hunter. I mean, I could stay, we could try and make it work but we both know it would fall apart eventually. I'm not good at relationships. I don't believe in love and I don't trust it. I know that I will never let myself love you because I'm terrified of giving myself over to something that won't last. And because my fear is bigger than anything, I will kill what we feel and you will end up hating me.

"And I can't live my life knowing you hate me, Hunt."

Hunt jammed his hands beneath his armpits and rocked on his heels. He looked away, and when he spoke again, he sounded miserable. "Don't walk out, Adie, don't go. Let's work this out."

Adie simply shook her head and pulled her bag out of the room, heading straight for his elevator. She glanced at the big Christmas tree in the corner of the sitting room, the hand-painted ornaments glinting in the morning light.

Happy damn Christmas to me.

This one, she decided, would probably be more miserable than all the rest put together.

Unfortunately, there was no one to blame but herself.

Ten

Adie had heard about receiving signs from a higher being but had always thought the universe had better things to do than send messages to inconsequential humans. But, sitting on the steps leading up to her flat in Notting Hill after a twenty-hour trip through hell, she was, maybe, starting to believe the New Agers might be onto something.

Because, damn, her flight from JFK had been a series of rolling disasters from start to finish. On her arrival at the airport, there had been, inexplicably, confusion about her ticket, with the computer not being able to find her booking. After finally receiving her boarding pass, she'd gone to the wrong gate and she'd heard only one call asking her to report for boarding, causing her to sprint to the other side of the terminal to make her flight. The airline attendants, and the passengers, hadn't been shy about expressing their irritation.

In the air, she'd thought her problems were over, but turbulence over the Atlantic had been brutal and then her plane had circled Heathrow for an hour before the pilot landed in a violent crosswind. On landing, she'd couldn't locate her luggage and, on finally reaching her flat—tearful and tired—she realized she'd lost her keys.

Well, not lost precisely, she recalled tipping out the contents of her bag in Hunt's apartment to swap bags and her keys must've fallen to the floor there.

She had a spare set of house keys in her desk drawer at work but the keys to her office were on the same ring as her keys to the flat. She needed her assistant, Kaycee, to let her into the office, but Kaycee was en-route to Dublin to spend Christmas with her family. She could call a locksmith but finding one would be near on impossible and if she did, she'd have to pay a king's ransom for his services. Another, less stressful option would be for her to find a hotel…

Or to go back to Manhattan…

The thought popped into her head, as it had done every minute since she'd stormed out of The Stellan. But this time she couldn't push it away, neither did she want to. She wanted to be in New York. Hunt, apparently, wanted her there…

Adie felt a drop of rain on her nose, then another. She glared up at the heavy sky. "Can you give me a break? I'm sitting, I'm thinking, I'm trying to work it out!"

Miraculously, someone upstairs was listening because the rain held off. Adie wrapped her arms around her knees and considered Hunt's proposal.

Okay, let's deal with the easy stuff first, she decided. Moving to Manhattan wouldn't be an issue, Kaycee was fantastically efficient and the majority of Adie's work was done over the internet. She'd have to fly back to London occasionally but that was why planes were invented.

Her parents wouldn't care where she lived, neither did they care what she did. They weren't a factor in her decision-making process.

Right, now she had to confront the thorny issue. Hunt…

No, Hunt wasn't the problem, *she* was.

He'd told her he wanted her to stay, that they had a chance of creating something amazing—a Christmas miracle in itself—and her first inclination was to dismiss his statement. Because, really, who fell in love in under a month?

Especially two people who didn't believe in love.

But Hunt, as he'd pointed out, was in his midthirties and he was a guy who knew his own mind. He wasn't one for overstating, for exaggeration. He meant what he said and said what he meant so, yeah, maybe he did want to make this work.

He hadn't said the words, but Adie thought he might love her. He wouldn't have given her false hope, mentioned her staying or having his babies if he didn't.

And falling in love with her was a helluva thing, given his history of loss and hurt and disappointment and his anti-commitment stance. If she weren't a yellow-bellied scaredy-cat, she'd be thrilled that a man like him—successful and powerful—had lowered his guard to let her into his life. He'd taken a chance, been brave, handed her his heart and his dreams and she'd stomped all over them in her high-heeled boots. Because she was scared.

She'd lived her life being scared—scared to be loved and have that love ripped away, scared to put her faith in someone to have them disappoint her time and time again. She didn't have enough courage to take a chance...

Your childhood is behind you, Adie...

How many times had she repeated those words to herself? But had she ever said them with any meaning? Her past, and her parents, were still dictating her actions today. She was still running instead of facing her problems. Her childhood was long over but she still let it influence her life. Her parents had been useless, neglectful and self-absorbed, but she didn't have to follow in their footsteps. She could do better, be better...

If she drilled down to the core of her feelings, if she pushed away her many excuses, denials and rationalizations, she knew she was utterly in love with Hunt. And yes, maybe they wouldn't last forever,

maybe everything would fall apart in two or three
months because that was what was destined to happen. But it wouldn't be because she created drama
or found a way to leave.

She was done with self-sabotaging.

She could only try.

Try, with everything she had, to be happy, to be
happy with Hunt.

Trying was all she could do. And that started with
getting back to New York…

Adie stood up, about to call for a ride, when a
ubiquitous London cab pulled to a smooth stop beside her. The window came down and the driver, who
looked remarkably like one of Santa's elves leaned
across the seat to give her a friendly grin. "Where
to, luv?"

"Heathrow?"

"Sure thing."

Adie climbed into the car and slammed the door
shut. Dragging her phone out of her bag, she quickly
jumped on the internet and saw that the next flight to
New York left in a few hours. She booked her ticket
and immediately got a message asking if she was
interested in being upgraded—free of charge—to
business class.

Uh, yes, please.

"You do know it's Christmas Eve, right?" The
driver asked her, looking at her in the rearview mirror. "The traffic is going to be hectic."

Adie smiled at him and shook her head. "We'll

be fine. In a matter of ten minutes, I've found you, booked a ticket, got an upgrade and look, the traffic is flowing freely."

"Well, huh. Guess the universe is looking out for you."

Adie smiled. Yep, maybe it was.

It was after midnight on Christmas Eve and Hunt walked down 5th Avenue with his hands jammed into his coat pockets and scowled at a couple taking a selfie in front of an overly decorated Christmas window. The woman lowered her phone, kissed her boyfriend and held up her phone again to catch their smooch.

He and Adie hadn't taken one photograph together. Hell, their relationship was over before either of them could think about keeping a memento of what they'd had.

And what was that? Hot sex over a few weeks...

Hunt tried to duck around a group of tourists standing in front of another window, but the crowd moved, forcing him to choose between staying where he was or stepping off the sidewalk into a puddle. Choosing to keep his feet dry, he looked over their heads into the window and immediately saw why it had captured the attention of the crowds.

It was a window within a window, posed mannequins looking at an old-fashioned winter wonderland scene, perfectly capturing Christmas. Even he, morose and sad and pissed, could appreciate the artistry in the window. The models were modern and stylish, sporting trendy clothing and accessories and the second window harked back to a simpler time, of tobogganing and snow, candy canes and enormous Christmas trees.

Adie would love the detail, the link between old and new.

Hunt turned away, wishing he could stop thinking about her, stop missing her. While only a day and a half had passed since she'd walked out, he could barely breathe because he missed her so much. He hadn't slept much last night, dozing off somewhere close to dawn only to wake up and reach for her...

To find she wasn't there. Hell of a thing to feel sucker punched as he opened his eyes, the air rushing from his lungs, feeling weak and shaky and so damn miserable.

Would he feel like this every morning for the rest of his life?

It'll fade, Hunt told himself. *It always does. This is just grief, you have to get through it, one day at a time. You've done it before, remember?*

As Kate said, he was a survivor.

His shoulders hunched against the icy wind, Hunt recalled Kate's words from his Christmas party a few nights ago.

"For Adie, love has been...elusive."

Hunt jerked to a stop, ignoring the "Watch it, dude" of a man who had to dodge him at the last minute.

Had he even told her that he loved her?

God, he couldn't remember.

He'd asked her to have a baby with him, to stay in New York, all but demanded it in fact. But had he told her that he loved her, that she was his world? Had he really, completely, fluently explained what she meant to him?

Would it have made a difference? Might she have considered…*more* had he uttered those three important words? Hunt preferred actions to words, but they'd had so little time together before they'd parted. Adie really didn't have time to realize that, while he was slow to commit, when he did commit, he went all in.

He didn't like to fail.

Even back in the day, as a young adult, when Joni had asked for a divorce, he'd wanted to stick it out. He'd worked his ass off, both as a player and in business, and success was always a certainty, not an option.

Did Adie realize that when he made a promise, when he set his mind on a task, he always, always gave it his all? Adie had no idea that his love wasn't conditional, that his loyalty was unshakeable. That he would love her through all her insecurities, that he was the one place where she would always and forever be adored, accepted? She hadn't had that as a child. Her parents had emotionally neglected her, but he wouldn't. It simply wasn't in his nature.

When he worked, he worked; when he loved he

loved. And he did love her. With everything he had, he was, with everything he could be.

Did she even have the faintest idea?

But how could she? They'd known each other for three weeks and the time they'd spent together outside the bedroom was minimal. He was a good lover but not that good, unfortunately.

He needed to tell her, now, *tonight*. Well, as soon as possible. He needed to explain, to lay all his cards on the table, to completely expose himself. He had to give everything he had to get her back.

She was worth it. She was worth anything.

Hunt yanked out his phone and scrolled through his phone, looking for the number of his pilot. Had Duncan filed it under *Pilot*, his name or the name of the airport where the plane was parked?

Forget it, he'd call Duncan. Hitting the one key on his keypad—idly noting that Duncan would soon be bumped to number two on his speed dial—he looked around and tried to get his bearings. Heading back in the direction of the old-fashioned window, he mentally urged Duncan to answer his damn phone.

"Hunter? It's late. Is everything okay?"

Hunt released the air he'd been holding. "Sorry, I know. But can you get hold of my pilot, tell him to file a flight plan to London? I want to leave first thing in the morning.

"And can you get Pete to collect me as soon as possible?"

"I'm on it," Duncan reassured him. He hesitated. "Is everything okay?"

"I'm not sure. Ask me that question in twenty-four to thirty-six hours," Hunt replied. Obstructed by the crowd by the window, he stepped off the sidewalk and his foot landed in a puddle, soaking his shoe and the bottom six inches of his pants.

Hunt winced at the cold before shrugging it off. It was only then that he remembered why Duncan wasn't in the city. "How's your friend?"

Duncan hesitated and then Hunt heard his long sigh. "Unchanged. I'm going to have to make a decision about whether to take him off life support or not."

"Jesus." Hunt rubbed his hand over his jaw, ashamed that he hadn't checked in on his assistant before now. "I'm so sorry, Duncan. Is there anything I can do?"

"No, but thank you," Duncan replied. "I might need some more time, Hunt. I thought I was over him, but I'm not, not really."

"You've got it," Hunt told him, his voice thick.

"Saying goodbye is hard and I'm regretting the things I said and so many of the things I didn't say."

Hunt heard the tears in Duncan's voice and tried to swallow the lump in his throat. He desperately looked for something to say that might offer comfort. "You were the person he trusted enough to make the big decisions for him, Duncan. He obviously loved you a great deal."

Duncan was silent for a long time and Hunter was okay with that. Sometimes it was simply enough to be connected, to have someone listen. Hunter heard him sniff but when Duncan spoke again, Hunt could tell he was back to his efficient self. "Flight plan, pilot, London, pick up ASAP. Got it."

"Merry Christmas, Duncan. I wish you... strength."

Duncan cleared his throat. "Merry Christmas, Hunter. And I hope she says yes."

How the hell did he know that? Hunter looked at his phone, but when he put it back to his ear to demand to know if his assistant had developed psychic powers, Duncan was gone.

And, yeah, Hunter hoped she said yes too.

Hunt brushed snow off his shoulders and stamped his feet as he stepped into the lobby of The Stellan, grateful for the blast of warmth. He looked toward the night doorman who'd lumbered to his feet.

"Mario, working Christmas Eve?"

"Yes, sir," Mario replied. "It's not a big deal, the family is only flying in later this morning."

"Nice," Hunt replied, wishing he could be certain of the reception from the only person—apart from the Williams clan—he considered his family.

Well, he'd soon know. In ten or so hours, he'd know whether Christmas would be his favorite holiday or if he'd be hating the holiday for the rest of his life.

"Pete will be here soon. Will you buzz me when he arrives?" Hunt asked, striding toward the elevator.

"Sure. But, Mr. Sheridan, you have a visitor."

Hunt sent him a sharp look, convinced that Mario had been at the Christmas eggnog when no one was looking. It was Christmas Eve, he lived alone and nobody would be visiting him at this time of night— or morning—at this time of the year.

Mario grinned at him, lifted his thumb and jerked it to the side. Hunt turned slowly and saw a small figure curled up on the visitor's couch in the lobby. Hunt's breathing turned shallow as he recognized that pale face, that messier-than-usual hair.

Adie.

Holy hell, she was back.

Hunt couldn't take his eyes off her. "When did she get in?"

"Shortly after you left," Mario replied. "She asked me not to call you, said that she'd wait for you to come home. I was about to call you when I noticed that she'd fallen asleep."

"She's been to the UK and back," Hunt said, trying to work out why she was in his lobby, back in his life. Did it matter? She was here.

Hope, warm and tentative, bloomed in his chest.

Mario chuckled. "So, are you going to just look at her or are you going to get her out of my lobby?"

"Out. But give me a second," Hunt answered, whipping out his phone. He quickly contacted Duncan and told him to cancel the flight plan and his driver.

Then Hunt bent over Adie, slid his hands and arms under her and gently lifted her to his chest. She stirred, her eyes fluttering open. "Hunt? Where am I?"

Hunt dropped a kiss in her hair. "Home, sweetheart. You're home."

"Good," Adie replied, before closing her eyes and falling back to sleep.

Adie opened her eyes and sat up. It was snowing again. Big fat flakes drifted past Hunt's huge bedroom window, one or two splattering against the glass. Dark heavy clouds told her that more snow was on the way, and the trees swaying in Central Park suggested the wind was howling.

Lying back down again, Adie decided it was a perfect day to drift back to sleep. She patted the bed next to her, but Hunt wasn't there. Maybe he'd gone to work…damn.

What was the time? Her watch was always where she left it, on the bedside table, and Adie picked it up and squinted at the face. It was past ten…

Well, huh. It had been a while since she'd slept so late. Adie peered over the side of the bed to see what she'd knocked to the floor when she picked up her watch and saw a bunch of keys, *her* bunch of keys. The ones that opened her flat and her offices…

She was back in New York…

Adie scampered out of bed, realizing that she was

dressed in one of Hunt's T-shirts. She glanced around the room to see her clothes piled up on the wingback chair next to his side of the bed.

Adie rubbed her forehead with the tips of her fingers as memories of the past thirty-six hours slapped her, hard and fast. It had been a smooth flight from London and she should've slept in the comfort of business class, but she'd been too hyped and far too nervous. It was only when she got to The Stellan and sat down on the couch in the lobby that she started to relax and she must've fallen asleep.

She presumed it was Hunt who got her upstairs, undressed her and put her to bed.

Where was he? Adie started to walk out of the bedroom to find him but then she caught a glimpse of herself in the mirror on the far wall and let out a tiny shriek. Her hair lay flat against her head on one side and stood up on the other, her face was creased from the pillow and her mascara dotted the tops of her lids and made tiny stripes under her eyes.

She looked like someone who'd been traveling for a couple of days. Oh, wait, she had been...

"God, get in the shower before he sees you," Adie told her reflection, grimacing.

"Too late," Hunt drawled from the doorway. "And I think you look amazing."

Adie whirled around and stared at him, drinking him in. He wore stone-gray chino pants and a white shirt under a crew neck sweater the color of a tangerine. Trendy sneakers covered his feet but it was his expression that captured her attention, part hope, part expectation, a little amusement.

She wanted to launch herself into his arms and was about to do that when she remembered that she needed to shower and brush her teeth. She placed her hand over her mouth and spoke through her fingers. "Hold that thought!"

At the door to his bathroom, she turned to look at him again. "Any chance of a coffee? And something to wear? Because I've lost my luggage. And can we talk?"

Hunt smiled at her erratic speech and nodded to the bedside table. "Coffee." Then he pointed to the dressing room. "Your bags arrived this morning. The airport had them delivered here because you put down my address as your primary residence. All your stuff is in the closet, your toiletries are in the bathroom."

Adie looked at the closet and then back at him. "You unpacked for me?"

"And I made a hell of a noise doing it." Hunt smiled. "I can't tell you how many times I nearly woke you up, but I couldn't, you were obviously exhausted."

Adie swayed from foot to foot, torn between wanting to get clean and stepping into his arms. Choosing to get her coffee, she took a huge sip, then another, sighing with pleasure.

Hunt slid his hands into the pockets of his pants. "Take a shower, Adie, and then we'll talk. But, if you are longer than ten minutes, I'll join you in there and trust me, no talking will be done."

It was tempting to linger but, Adie thought as she brushed her teeth, the next time they made love she didn't want any misunderstandings between them.

Hopefully, she'd be in his arms, in his bed soon because, really, how long did it take to say sorry, I was wrong, I love you and please can I stay?

Hunt heard her footsteps coming down the hallway and turned away from the window in his sitting room. She couldn't have been more than fifteen minutes, but it seemed longer, an age. God, she looked amazing and he couldn't believe she was here, in his apartment.

He took a moment to study her, pleased she hadn't taken the time to apply makeup or dry her newly washed hair. She'd pulled on yoga pants and a thigh-length sweater and her feet were bare. Her lack of fussing suggested she was as eager to get things settled as he was.

And he couldn't wait so he jumped straight in.

"Why did you come back, Adie?"

Adie perched on the edge of the cushion of his leather couch, placing her hands between her knees. Hunt sat down opposite her, his forearms on his knees, his eyes locked on hers.

"I had a nightmare trip back to London, everything went wrong. I got back to my apartment and realized I'd lost my flat keys."

"I found them next to the bed," Hunt replied.

"I thought about going to a hotel but quickly realized that wasn't where I wanted to be."

Hunt, desperate to pull the words out of her, forced himself to be patient, to wait for her to explain in her own way. They had only one shot at this and he wanted to get it right.

Adie sighed. "My default setting is to run when a guy tells me I'm important. Normally I run only after things are a little more established, after I've driven him to distraction and found an excuse to bail. I don't trust myself when it comes to love, Hunt. And, normally, I find it impossible to trust a man when he says that he loves me. I guess that's because my parents blithely and frequently told me they loved me, but I knew they didn't because their actions didn't match up to their words."

She said normally, *hang onto that word.*

Hunt linked his hands together, riding the waves of emotion. Anger at her parents, love and tenderness and protectiveness for her.

Adie looked at him as if expecting him to say something, but he just rolled his index finger in the air, silently telling her to continue.

It took a little time for her to speak again. "When I got to London, I realized that it's not you I don't trust, it's me." She pulled in a deep breath and met his eyes. "I'm hoping you are in love with me. I know that I'm in love with you—I have been since that night I first met you."

"Thank God," Hunt muttered.

Adie held up her hand. "I'm so damn scared, Hunt." She stared down at her intertwined fingers, which were as white as his own. He flexed his fingers and felt blood rushing back to his digits. Standing, he walked around the coffee table that separated them and sat down on its glass top. Adie released an agitated squawk and swatted his knee.

"Get off, it'll break. That's a limited edition table."

"It's strong and it will hold me and I don't give a damn how expensive it is," Hunt stated. And it was true, she was all that was important.

And taking that fear out of her eyes was also imperative. Hunt placed his hands on her knees and squeezed. "Love is a scary emotion. And because I'm very much in love with you, I'm equally terrified."

"You are?" Adie asked, obviously surprised. "I didn't think anything could scare you."

"You terrify me. Losing you terrifies me. Confession time, when I found you in the lobby, I was heading upstairs to pack a bag. I was going to follow you to London."

Adie's big eyes slammed into his. "You were?"

He lifted his hand to stroke her cheekbone. "I was prepared to beg you into coming back with me." He needed a clear answer, then he could breathe easily again. "Are you back, Adie?"

Adie nodded, tears in her eyes. Hunt was about to grab her, to haul her to him, when she held up her hand again. "You should know that I'm not good at being in a relationship, Hunt, but I'm going to try. I love you too much not to try and you've got to promise not to give up on me."

He'd never give up on her. He started what he finished, as he now informed her.

Adie smiled at his reassurance, but he could tell that she still wasn't convinced.

She hesitated before speaking again. "I'm not opposed to having a family, to kids, to making a solid commitment, but can we take it one step at a time? We've only known each other such a short time and it's all gone so fast."

Hunt considered her question and was about to tell her he'd give her as much time as she wanted when a small voice deep inside him told him not to. Trusting his instinct, he shook his head. "Nope, that's not going to happen. I'm not going to give you any time to talk yourself out of this, to let your head override your heart.

"I want to get married, now, immediately. By New Year's Eve at the latest. And then I want us to ditch the contraception," Hunt added.

Adie's mouth dropped open and she was the loveliest goldfish Hunt had ever seen. "No, Hunt, we can't!"

Hunt smiled at her. "We can and we will. Come on, Adie, jump all in with me, take this massive leap of faith. Be bold, be courageous."

Adie started to laugh. *"Hunter..."*

"Adie. Yes or no? Will you marry me immediately?" Hunt made sure she heard the serious question behind his smile. "Love me, sweetheart, and let me love you as you've never been loved before."

Adie rested her fist against her lips. "You're being serious."

"Deadly," Hunt said, desperate for an answer. "Well?"

He saw her haul in a breath and for one second, just one, he thought she might say no, but then her smile bloomed, her eyes danced and she lifted her shoulders in a carefree shrug. A low chuckle rumbled out of her. "What the hell…okay. Tie me up in knots, Sheridan, tie me up so tight that I can't run. So tight that all I can do is love you."

Hunt leaned forward and his lips brushed hers. "That's all I want, Adie, is for you to love me."

Adie draped her arms around his neck and looked into his eyes, love and desire and relief rolling through hers. "I do. So much."

Hunt rested his forehead against hers, his hands still gripping her knees. "And I love you, darling. Welcome home."

And, judging by her tender expression, Hunt knew she finally accepted that he—not this building or this city—was her home, with him was where she was meant to be.

Just like she was his soft place to fall.

It was, he decided, going to be an exceptionally good Christmas after all.

* * * * *

*No one gets under Jackson Cooper's skin like
Cricket Maxfield. When he goes all in at a charity
poker match, Jackson loses their bet and becomes her
reluctant ranch hand. In close quarters, tempers
flare—and the fire between them ignites into a
passion that won't be ignored...*

Read on for a sneak peek at
The Rancher's Wager
by New York Times *bestselling author Maisey Yates!*

Cricket Maxfield had a hell of a hand. And her confidence made
that clear. Poor little thing didn't think she needed a poker face if
she had a hand that could win.

But he knew better.

She was sitting there with his hat, oversize and over her eyes, on
her head and an unlit cigar in her mouth.

A mouth that was disconcertingly red tonight, as she had clearly
conceded to allowing her sister Emerson to make her up for the
occasion. That bulky, fringed leather jacket should have looked
ridiculous, but over that red dress, cut scandalously low, giving a
tantalizing wedge of scarlet along with pale, creamy cleavage, she
was looking not ridiculous at all.

And right now, she was looking like far too much of a winner.

Lucky for him, around the time he'd escalated the betting, he'd
been sure she would win.

He'd wanted her to win.

"I guess that makes you my ranch hand," she said. "Don't worry.
I'm a very good boss."

Now, Jackson did not want a boss. Not at his job, and not in his
bedroom. But her words sent a streak of fire through his blood. Not
because he wanted her in charge. But because he wanted to show
her what a boss looked like.

Cricket was…

A nuisance. If anything.

That he had any awareness of her at all was problematic enough. Much less that he had any awareness of her as a woman. But that was just because of what she was wearing. The truth of the matter was, Cricket would turn back into the little pumpkin she usually was once this evening was over and he could forget all about the fact that he had ever been tempted to look down her dress during a game of cards.

"Oh, I'm sure you are, sugar."

"I'm your boss. Not your sugar."

"I wasn't aware that you winning me in a game of cards gave you the right to tell me how to talk."

"If I'm your boss, then I definitely have the right to tell you how to talk."

"Seems like a gray area to me." He waited for a moment, let the word roll around on his tongue, savoring it so he could really, really give himself all the anticipation he was due. "Sugar."

"We're going to have to work on your attitude. You're insubordinate."

"Again," he said, offering her a smile, "I don't recall promising a specific attitude."

There was activity going on around him. The small crowd watching the game was cheering, enjoying the way this rivalry was playing out in front of them. He couldn't blame them. If the situation wasn't at his expense, then he would have probably been smirking and enjoying himself along with the rest of the audience, watching the idiot who had lost to the little girl with the cigar.

He might have lost the hand, but he had a feeling he'd win the game.

Don't miss what happens next in…
The Rancher's Wager
by New York Times *bestselling author Maisey Yates!*

Available January 2021 wherever
Harlequin Desire books and ebooks are sold.

Harlequin.com